FOXCOVER
DICK CATE

ILLUSTRATED BY
CAROLINE BINCH

YEARLING BOOKS

FOXCOVER

A YEARLING BOOK 0 440 862140

Originally published in Great Britain by Victor Gollancz Ltd.

First publication in Great Britain

PRINTING HISTORY
Victor Gollancz edition published 1988
Yearling edition published 1989

This book is set in 14/16 pt Century Schoolbook

Yearling Books are published by Transworld Publishers Ltd.,
61–63 Uxbridge Road, Ealing, London W5 5SA, in Australia by
Transworld Publishers (Australia) Pty. Ltd., 15–23 Helles
Avenue, Moorebank, NSW 2170, and in New Zealand by
Transworld Publishers (N.Z.) Ltd., Cnr. Moselle and Waipareira
Avenues, Henderson, Auckland.

Made and printed in Great Britain by
The Guernsey Press Co. Ltd., Guernsey, Channel Islands.

FOXCOVER

Chapter 1

Butch scrambled up onto the biggest boulder and glared back down at Billy. When he whacked his stick on the rock the sound echoed like pistol shots.

All the Gang were in their secret den in the abandoned tunnel of the limestone quarry. All of them except Joey White: he'd been booted out last week.

And after what had just happened, Billy had the feeling that he'd be the next one to get the order of the boot.

'I want no more back-answers from you, Robinson!' Butch spat out. 'I'm pig sick of you! That clear?'

The tunnel lent his voice a funny sound – like one of the cave oracles Mrs Drury was always boring them silly with when she talked about the Greek myths.

'Aye-aye, cap'n!' said Elvis and he popped the bubble gum he'd just swiped from Cloughy.

'Let's gerron with the plan,' growled Butch, still glaring down at Billy. 'Any suggestions?'

'Why don't we rob the Midland Bank instead?' asked Elvis.

'Don't talk stupid!' said Butch, glaring down at him now, for a change.

Elvis grinned back at him and popped another bubble. He was sitting on the packing case that was supposed to be their conference table. He was probably reckoning on taking the packing case home with him tonight, because the Potters hadn't a stick of furniture left in their house.

Last week they'd had a houseful but Mr Potter had put all his dole money on a horse called One Leg Larry and lost the lot. It wasn't the first time. Furniture had a tendency to come and go in the Potter household: sofas, carpets, cocktail cabinets, tellies, videos flowed in and out like the tides. Not that Mrs Potter was worried. Last night she'd told Billy she'd just as soon curl up on a doormat any day of the week as lie down on a divan. And Mr Potter never noticed what he was sitting on. Sometimes he even sat on the dog.

'How much did One Leg Larry lose by?' Billy had asked Elvis when they were walking down to the quarry together.

'Seven furlongs,' Elvis had said.

'How far was the race?'

'Six.'

You could never get any sense out of him.

'How far's a furlong?' Billy had asked him as they turned into the quarry entrance.

'How fur's a farlong?' Elvis had replied. 'Fur enough!'

He was mad. Maybe that was why he got away with murder.

Not like some people.

All Billy had said was that tomorrow – Saturday – he'd rather play football than go down Doggy Wood and wreck the Crag Enders' camp, and Butch had jumped feet first down his throat with his boots on. He hadn't jumped down Daz's throat five minutes before when *he'd* suggested the same thing. In any case, it was the only sensible thing to do, really, with the match with Middleham coming up.

'SHUT YER BIG CAKEHOLE ROBINSON!' Butch had bellowed – like a bull.

Billy had felt a right twit. Cloughy had giggled behind his back. He'd have slapped Cloughy down, like he'd done last week, only he thought he'd better not. Even Daz had said nothing, and he was supposed to be keen on football.

Billy knew what was the matter, of course. All this had started because he'd spoken up for Joey over the frog business down at the marshes last week. Butch didn't like people speaking up. He preferred them to shut up instead: bow down before him. Say *Master, master!*

And he hadn't liked what Billy had said at the football meeting with Miss Benfold, either: but Billy was glad he'd said it now, even though Emma Ward *was* only a girl.

Point was, Butcher was nuts.

It was nuts, for example, what he was talking about now.

He'd switched to going on about their Lookout Post in Foxcover Wood. Slattery – in the top class – was supposed to have told him the Crag Enders were going to attack it again. What did Slattery know about it, anyhow? Why was he always shoving his big oar in?

'What we want is a guard on it,' Butch was saying. 'A twenty-four hour guard.'

9

He was only calling it that because his brother had been in the Falklands. He'd got a medal from the government and now they'd sent him out to Northern Ireland.

Couple of weeks ago he'd been playing football with them down at the rec, when he was on leave. He hadn't been a bad player. Better than Butcher. At least he didn't have two left feet. When Butch tried to beat you he *always* went to his right.

'Nobody sets foot from now on in Foxcover,' Butch was saying. 'It's our property.'

Nuts, baloney, and bananas.

Billy looked down and shook his head, slightly.

Foxcover belonged to nobody now, Mr Wainwright had told Billy that. It had belonged to the railway company that put the Old Line through from Shilton Colliery to the station, but that was in the old days. Now Mr Morgan was trying to get it for his farm. He wanted a grant from the EEC to chop the trees down and plant oilseed rape instead.

'An' if they do we punish them,' Butch said.

'Good idea,' said Elvis. 'Shoot them first, then punish them after. Shoot Chuffy an' all.'

'What for, Elvis?' asked Little Chuff grinning up at him.

'Cos I'm sick of you punchin' people around!'

Little Chuff grinned up at him, trying to get the joke. He was an underfed runt who couldn't have punched his way out of a paper bag if he'd tried. His big sister, Patricia, was the same. Neither of them had much sense. People said their dad had totally knocked whatever sense they'd ever had

10

out of them. He was forever handing out a bit of fist. The cruelty to children people had been round twice. On cold nights he kept locking Patricia and Chuffy out in the yard.

'We ought to mek a rota,' said Butch.

Another army word! Another bunch of bananas.

How could a rota work? Who was going to do it tonight, for instance, for a start off, when *The Bobby Downes Spectacular* was on?

Billy never missed *The Bobby Downes Spectacular*. Nobody in their right senses would. Because it was quite simply the best show that had ever been on the telly. Every time he met a pretty girl Bobby's trousers fell down and then jerked straight back up again because they must have been on elastic. He always had Union Jack underpants with words printed on that said *This is the end* or *I support the government*.

'Good idea,' said Cloughy.

It was all so daft!

Billy knew he shouldn't say anything.

But he had to. You couldn't listen to drivel *all* your life.

'It's all daft!' he said.

'EH?'

'I mean, who's gonna do—'

He didn't get any further.

The words dried up in his throat because Butch had scrambled down from his throne and was rushing towards him.

11

Chapter 2

'Smell that!' said Butch. He shoved his fist right under Billy's nose. 'Fancy a taste, Robinson?'

Elvis would have replied with something really witty like, *No thanks, I've just had me tea* or *We're particular what we eat in our house.*

But Billy didn't say anything like that.

He didn't say anything at all.

'Thought not!' said Butch, smirking down at him.

He turned and strode away, shouldering his stick like a soldier's rifle, and clambered back up to where he'd come from.

Billy felt even more of a fool now.

He wished he'd spoken up, instead of standing there like a dumb cluck. But it had all happened so quick. It wasn't that he'd been scared, not really.

He could hear Cloughy sniggering away behind him again. Then a clump. Probably Elvis whopping him one.

Then Elvis said:

'Gettin' sick and tired of all this jawing. If we gonna wreck their den, what for we don't shoot off down Doggy Wood and do it now?'

'If we do, he's not coming!' said Butch, nodding down at Billy.

'Robbo's okay, man, Butch,' said Daz.

'Who give you permission to speak all of a sudden, fancy-pants? Don't know the first thing about scrappin', you don't!'

Which was more or less true. Daz was brilliant at dribbling a ball, but not keen on fights. One good punch and he was ready to retire hurt.

'So shut yer great big cakehole!' said Butch. 'He's an M.L.B.'

'What's an M.L.B?' Chuffy asked.

'Mother's Little Baby,' Elvis explained to him. 'Wish they'd learn you kids summat at that school!'

The stick whacked on the rock.

'That's what you are, Robinson! Mother's Little Baby!'

Butch was saying that because last week Billy's mother wouldn't let him watch the Saturday night horror movie. It was about a man who worked in a laboratory and he put what he thought was some milk in his tea, and it wasn't, and he turned into a giant tapeworm and started eating everybody. It must have been a really great film. Everybody in the school had been allowed to watch it, even Chuffy and his sister. Except Billy and Samantha Soskiss, that is. Soskiss had to do her fiddle lesson instead.

Billy shook his head.

'Eh? Lass-lad? Speak up! I'm deaf an' I can't hear you!'

Before Billy spoke there was a pause that seemed to last a century.

'That's not right, man, Butch,' said Billy.

He could hardly hear the words. He could hardly get them out.

'What isn't right, Lass-lad?'

'What you just said.'

'What'd I just say, Lass-lad?'

'About M.L.B.'

Billy's throat was getting drier all the time.

'What about it?'

Billy could hear stupid Cloughy giggling again. He couldn't trust himself to speak.

'Don't know what we've got you in the Gang for, William Robinson!'

That was what Mrs Drury sometimes called him. She'd called him that this afternoon when Billy had got top marks for his essay on Cadmus. Butch had sniggered behind his hand as if he could hardly stop laughing.

'Come to the front, William Robinson, and read out your winning story,' Mrs Drury had said.

Billy had felt proud and scared at the same time as he read aloud his story about how Cadmus and his brothers had been driven from the land because they had allowed a white bull (really a god who had come down to earth) to run off with their sister Europa.

So Cadmus and his brothers and their mother the queen went out into the dark of night and began their lonely wanderings. Wherever would it lead to next? his story had ended.

Everybody had clapped. Even Samantha Soskiss, who usually won everything.

But Billy had known Butch was sniggering behind his hand all the time.

'No wonder you don't want to go down Doggy Wood!' said Butch. Obviously a thought had struck him. 'Because you're no good at fighting!'

'He beat Cloughy last week,' said Daz.

'I've warned you, Monster-mouth!'

He stared down at Daz until he looked away. He loved that. Eyeballing people. Humiliating them.

Then he switched his glare back to Billy.

'You couldn't beat an egg – William Robinson!' Big joke. Ha! Ha!

'That meks you less than an egg. Cloughy,' said Elvis.

'Eh?'

'Don't you get it, Cloughy-duffy? Are you that thick? If Billy beats you and he can't beat an egg it means you're less than an egg! Gerrit now, Duffy? Needn't worry, though, 'cos you're cracked!'

'I'll crack you in a minute, Elvis!' said Butch. His face was as red as a balloon. When he was quite sure Elvis was buttoned up, he turned his gaze back to Billy again. 'I say you're a Mother's Little Baby, William Robinson. What do you say to that?'

Billy shook his head again.

'You contradictin' me?'

Billy didn't answer. He heard Butch scrambling down the boulder. Heard him toss aside his big stick, heard it clatter on the rocks. Then he was standing in front of Billy. Going into his Great Eyeball Act.

'You want a fight, Robinson?'

Billy didn't say anything. Who in their right senses wanted a fight with Butcher?

He wanted to smile, look calm, like Joey had done last week. But he couldn't. He felt worried inside, and cold. He tried his best to look Butch in the eye, but couldn't even do that. He wished he could think of the right words to say. He wanted to swallow, to clear his throat. It was daft trying to fight somebody like Butch. It wasn't that he was scared, not really, but—

'I'm waiting, Robinson!'

'Everybody knows you're the best fighter, man, Butch,' said Daz.

'I HAVE WARNED YOU, MONSTER-MOUTH!' Then, turning back to Billy, more quietly, 'What you say, Robinson?'

Cloughy sniggered. 'I bet anything Butch could beat Leon Leroy,' he said.

Leon Leroy was the British heavyweight champion and every month he fought an American Beer-belly. He was built like a wardrobe, only with longer arms. He was on telly tonight, fighting American Beer-belly Number Six.

'Who's Leon Leroy?' Chuffy asked.

'Chap down our street that breeds whippets,' Elvis explained.

'I am waiting!'

Billy held on for a few moments more, then lowered his eyes to the ground.

17

'Thought you were chicken! Knew all along! He's chicken! We want no chickens in this gang, William Robinson. You better join Emma Ward! She'll be waiting for you outside! Off you go, Lasslad!'

Chapter 3

Billy was halfway across the floor of the quarry before he realised where he was. He must have walked twenty yards, yet he couldn't remember a single step!

He couldn't even remember coming out into the quarry. The light of day always hit you when you came out of the darkness of the tunnel. But this time he couldn't remember it at all.

Maybe it was because there was a light inside his head. A red, glaring light.

He skirted round a big pond.

He'd be like Joey White. *He* didn't seem to mind being out of the Gang. Billy only wished he'd stood up to Butch a bit more, like Joey had. Joey had taken the frog that Cloughy had caught and when Butch handed him the stone to kill it he just smiled right up into Butch's face.

'Don't want to, man,' he'd said. 'What you want to kill a little frog for, man?'

'Because I say so!' Butch had said.

'Initiation test,' said Slattery, who hated Joey.

'That's right,' said Butch.

So in reply Joey had dropped the frog into a deep pool, where it was safe, and smiled up at the pair of them.

Even when Butch had punched him and he fell in the water, even when Butch chucked him out of the Gang, he'd still kept smiling.

Billy wished *he'd* managed to do that.

'Hoo, man!'

It was Daz. Standing in the entrance to the tunnel. Looking back at him Billy realised for the first time that his eyes were full of tears. Daz, the quarry face, the gorse bushes topping it, the sky above that were all blurred and watery.

'Want us to come wi' you?'

Billy shook his head and turned away.

He didn't want anybody to see him crying like this.

He waited till he was passing behind the quarrymen's hut before he wiped his eyes with his sleeve.

When he reached the part where the quarry opened onto the Old Line he looked back. He could see the entrance to the tunnel again now. Daz was still there. Billy waved at him. Daz waved back, then disappeared into the den.

Just like him!

Billy wiped his eyes again. Made certain they were dry. Emma Ward would be just round the corner. Always trying to get in the Gang. Always following him around.

The other day he'd been in one of the bogs at school and got the fright of his life when he'd seen somebody had written the word ROBINSON on the back of the door. At first it didn't worry him. But what if they were going to add something else, and got disturbed? He'd tried to rub it out, but it was one of these indelible pens. Slattery had pinched one of Mr Fixby's, everybody knew.

In a way it was all Emma Ward's fault. He

should never have opened his big trap at the football meeting. It was true she was a good footballer. But when all was said and done, she *was* only a girl. And it wasn't only skill you needed at football.

He'd been right. She was there, five yards up the bankside among some dock plants and tall yellow weeds.

'What's up, Billy?' she asked as he came towards her.

As if she didn't know!

He didn't look up as he passed her. Kept his head down, seeing only the overgrown sleepers of the old railway line.

It surprised him how much he hated her all of a sudden.

'What's up, Billy?' she asked again as he left her behind.

He didn't answer. He didn't want to answer.

He didn't ever want to speak to her again.

'Have you come out of the Gang?'

She had climbed down on to the Old Line now and was walking behind him. What did she want to do that for?

'Butch is mad,' she called after him.

He walked on.

'Billy!'

He started to climb up the path of the waste heap at the side of Mr Fletcher's allotment. Everybody called it his ranch. He kept pigs and ducks and goats and lived all by himself in an old railway carriage because years ago he'd lost his wife, Billy's grandma had told him.

22

'Totally cut himself off, Billy,' she'd said.

Billy would be like that, from now on.

One of Rancher Fletcher's goats shook its head and baa-ed as that thought went through Billy's head.

What did a goat know about it! What did anybody? It was all senseless.

'Billy!' shouted Emma behind him.

He ignored her.

Chapter 4

Who did Butcher think he was, anyway? Just because his brother had a blinking medal! What about Uncle Ronnie?

Billy smiled when he thought of his Uncle Ronnie. He felt one up on Butcher. He'd never actually met Uncle Ronnie, never would. Ever since he could remember his photo had stood on his grandma's sideboard smiling out at them all. But in a way Billy felt he knew him better than lots of people still alive.

And it was a fact Uncle Ronnie had gone one stage better than just winning a medal!

As he turned down the backs one thought became crystal clear in Billy's mind. He was going to get his revenge on Cliffy Butcher. Definitely.

Nobody makes a fool of me and gets away with it, he thought.

It was a line from a cowboy film he'd seen last week. The young hero had said it after he'd been made a fool of in a bar. Years later the young hero shot the toughie in a fair fight and became famous.

But nobody! thought Billy.

He might have to wait a long time. But he'd do it in the end.

He paused outside the back gate to make sure his eyes were dry – then pushed it open and went across the yard.

Mr Brunsdon, the union man at the factory where Billy's dad worked, was sitting at their kitchen table when he went in.

'I tell you, man, Dick,' he was saying to Billy's dad, 'there's bound to be trouble.'

'How d'you mek that out?' asked Billy's dad. He was at the sink having a sluice-down after work. Billy's mam was sitting at the table across from Mr Brunsdon looking like death-warmed-up.

'If we don't do summat fast they gonna shut that place down in a fortnight – that's what they're after! There's got to be war, Dick!'

Mr Brunsdon rested his meaty fist on the table and leaned back in his chair, nearly crushing the poor thing to death. In his younger days he had wrestled under the name of The Belton Brute.

'I fail to see what good all this talk about war's going to do, Matty.' said Billy's mam.

'It's not the matter of good, Mrs Robinson.' Mr Brunsdon screwed round in his chair. 'It's a matter of rights. Nobody wants war. None of us—'

'I'm not so sure meself,' said Billy's mam. 'Personally speaking, like, I think some folks like fighting!'

'But like I say, if war's what they want, war's what they'll get!'

When he said that he clenched his big fist and Billy could just imagine it crushing to death the new cricket ball that Miss Benfold kept locked up in her gym-cupboard.

Whatever had possessed him to mention Wardy's name to Miss Benfold? He must have been out of his tiny mind. He'd know better next time!

'I'm against violence, Matty,' said Billy's dad, who had just finished rinsing his face. Billy's mam handed him a towel and he dabbed his face dry. 'You know that. I told you when we had all that carry-on at the pit. And I see no reason to change my mind now.'

'We're all against violence, Dick!' said Mr Brunsdon. 'Do you think *I* want violence?'

Billy's dad didn't say anything. He just looked hard at Mr Brunsdon.

'But the point is this, Dick,' Mr Brunsdon said. 'They're going to do the dirty on us. This factory's been open not much longer than a year, and now they're going to shut it down. Then what? Where else is there to work round here? You tell me! Eh? That's why we all need to pull together and put our foot down hard – now – while the iron's hot – before it blossoms into summat fresh. That's why we need men like you and Tommy Butcher.' That was Butch's dad. 'Fellers wi' a bit of experience.'

'Has Archie Hyslop sent you round here?'

'Eh? Archie never mentioned your name, Dick, I swear to God.'

You could tell he was lying.

'Because you know what my opinion is of Archie Hyslop!'

'You misjudge the man totally, Dick.'

'Buy you at one end of the street and sell you at the other!'

Archie Hyslop was the secretary in the local union. He was always on the telly.

'Union man through and through,' said Mr Brunsdon.

Billy's mam snorted.

'Archie Hyslop's not using me like he's been using Tommy Butcher,' said Billy's dad.

'Eh? What? What's Tommy Butcher supposed to be doin'?'

'You know nicely what he's up to – at Hyslop's behest!'

'Tommy Butcher's always been one for trouble!' said Billy's mam.

'I'll remind you it was Tommy Butcher held the strike together at the pit, missus,' said Mr Brunsdon, rounding on her and inflicting punishment on the chair again.

'And where did that get us?' asked Billy's dad.

'Exactly nowhere!' said his mam.

'Exactly my point, Mrs Robinson,' said Mr Brunsdon, jabbing a stubby finger straight at her, his eyes lighting up with anger. 'Like Archie Hyslop was saying to us last night, if we don't all stick together in the same boat now we'll end up sinking – and then mebbies there'll be *no* jobs round here for any of us to go to! Bear that in mind!' He kept jabbing his fat finger at her the whole time. 'In the end there'll be that many dole offices round here they'll have to import foreign labour to give out the dole!'

'Don't point your finger like that at my wife, Matty,' said Billy's dad. He wasn't a big man, but he could be terribly awkward. You could tell that from the look in his eyes.

'Eh? What?'

'The wife might not like it, Matty – being pointed at.'

27

'Eh? Oh! I'm sorry, Mrs Robinson, no offence intended.' Mr Brunsdon leaned back in his chair and nearly wrecked it. You could tell he wasn't over-pleased, but he tried his best to smile.

Billy's mam sniffed.

'To my way of thinking,' said Billy's dad, 'there'll be no jobs left anyhow. Whatever we do.' He was buttoning his shirt down the front. 'That's the way I see it.'

'True enough. But if we do summat now we might have a chance. What do you say, Dick? We need a few fellers like you and Tommy Butcher to make this strike stick. These young fellers haven't a clue. Are you for us or against us?'

'If the union calls a strike, I'll strike,' said Billy's dad. 'I've always been a good union man.'

'And you'll mek yourself available for picketing?'

'If the union asks me to picket, I'll picket.'

'Good enough.'

'But not wi' a pick-shaft in me hand. I don't want no carry-on like we had at the pit.'

'Good God, man, Dick, do you think we're a load of barbarians?'

'Just as long as that's understood,' said Billy's dad.

Chapter 5

Soon as Mr Brunsdon had gone Billy and his dad went into the other room. They always watched the news on telly while Billy's mam got the supper ready.

'What's Mr Butcher been up to, Dad?' Billy asked.

'Never you mind,' his dad said.

'Nothing good!' his mother shouted from the kitchen.

She was narked because it looked like they were going on strike, even though the top men down in London had told them not to.

Billy was glad his dad was going on strike. He'd noticed how Mr Brunsdon didn't think they could manage without fellers like his dad. That made him feel proud. His dad was always in demand down the Club for refereeing pool matches and bowls matches. He was known to be fair-minded and 'straight'.

And Billy was beginning to feel happier about what had happened down in the den. If he'd bothered to stand up to Butcher he could probably have beaten him easy. He'd just had three fights with Butcher – in his imagination – and won easy every time. Butcher was probably a walk-over, really. Just a big-gob.

Who needed gangs, anyway? Gangs were just stupid when you thought about them.

The news was on now. Same old stuff. There was a street in some city in the Middle East with an ambulance wailing down it. A block of flats had been blown up. A hole in a wall looked like a giant fist had smashed through it. An Arab was saying his men would never leave the city until they had won their struggle for their homeland.

It was typical of stupid Butcher to think of nothing better than wrecking the Crag Enders' den!

'We are winning,' the Arab said. He looked tired and weary. For weeks his men had been pushed further and further back by their enemies. Now they were cornered in a small part of the city.

As for Emma Ward, it made him mad when he thought about her. No wonder Miss Benfold looked surprised. He only hoped it didn't stop his chances of being captain. Miss Benfold had hinted he might be.

Princess Diana was on now, opening a children's wing in a hospital. The reporter was going on about her dress and matching hat. The dress was long and blue, and reached right down to her ankles. Last week it had been above her knees. 'Certain to create a new trend,' said the reporter. The hat was a funny shape, thin, with a split on top, perched on the side of her head as if it was going to slide off at any minute. Where had he seen a hat like that before? Last Christmas Billy's sister, Sandra, had paid fifteen quid of good money to have her hair cut exactly like Princess Diana as part of her present from her husband,

Steven. She was daft like that. Where *had* he seen that hat? He knew it was somewhere.

His mam had come in from the kitchen to watch Princess Diana. She always did when somebody in the royal family came on telly. Billy was more like his dad, not fussed either way about royalty.

But when cricket came on she stayed in the doorway, watching. That wasn't like her. Come to think of it, Billy couldn't smell anything cooking. He couldn't remember hearing pans banging or water shushing into them.

'What's up, lass?' asked Billy's dad. 'Summat wrong?'

'You know nicely what's wrong.'

'I don't.' He reached for his pipe and lit it.

'So that's it, is it?' she said. 'You're going on strike again, are you?'

'Look's like it, lass.' Billy's dad kept looking at the telly.

'I thought you told me the executive was against it?'

'What do them down London know about what's going on up here, Alice?'

Billy hoped his mam wasn't going to start a row, not just when there were some pictures of England thrashing the Aussies, for once!

'That means no money coming in the house again.'

'Likely as not.'

'In that case I might as well get a job myself.'

'You won't, Alice!'

She'd wanted to get a job the last time Billy's dad had been on strike, but he'd stopped her. She had worked in the food-kitchens, though, serving out the free meals to the miners and their families.

'What for?'

'We've been all over this before, Alice. You'll not get a job as long as you live in this house.'

'Why not? Am I not good enough?'

'It's not a question of that, is it? What sort of job would you end up with?'

'Who's going to fetch the money in, then?'

'I'm not having a wife of mine skivvying for other folk.'

'What else do I do here but skivvy?'

She went into the kitchen, what to do Billy couldn't imagine, she didn't make a sound.

The weatherman came on, the one with jam-jar specs, the one everybody liked. You couldn't understand everything he said because he had a funny accent and mumbled, but at least he gave you a laugh.

'All this mumble weather is coming to a mumble,' he said, 'and sure as fate this deepening depression is heading in our mumble direction! So it's wellies time again and mumble jumble, though always bear in mind that however mumble jumble it is it's probably a wee bit mumbler in mid-Atlantic!'

He flashed his glasses and paused for the laugh.

Usually Billy's dad gave him one. But not this time.

If anything his face looked grimmer than the weather forecast.

Chapter 6

After that things went from bad to rotten.

Billy knew it was really serious because his mam wouldn't come out of the kitchen, even for her favourite soap opera.

'Let's have the telly off now,' said his dad. 'We don't want to sit and watch it all night.'

Billy only hoped it was going to go on again in time for *The Bobby Downes Spectacular*.

By seven Billy could hear his dad's stomach making more noise than a shipwrecked volcano. The dog started to whine in sympathy, and even the Murrays next door must have heard it.

His dad had one of these regular stomachs which got upset if it didn't get fed at the usual time and went into a state of widespread public protest if it didn't get taken down to the Club at the usual time for its pint of beer.

At eight he told Billy to go for some fish and chips.

'I don't want any, mind!' said his mam from the kitchen.

'What for, lass?'

'Because I don't.'

'You'll have to eat summat, woman. If there's nothing in your belly you'll starve!'

'I'll just have to starve.'

'Get a shift on, then, Billy,' said his dad.

* * *

Elvis saw Billy coming and waited at the end of Chapel Row for him.

'What's up wi' you?'

He knew that in Billy's house they only had chips on Saturday night.

Billy told him about his mam and dad.

'Me dad and Our Soss's rowing an' all,' said Elvis.

'What about this time?'

Soss had been talking to the people who'd moved into Scott's bakery. They called it a commune. They all wore Ban the Bomb badges. All the women had long skirts, and all the men had long beards. Her dad didn't like it because he reckoned they were communists, and he'd told Soss not to go there again.

'What did your Soss say?'

'Told me dad to get stuffed.'

Nothing like that ever happened in Billy's house.

The boxing match was just starting when they went in the chip shop. Leon Leroy was showing off his muscles to the camera (he had muscles where other people had brains) and his opponent, the American beer-belly, was resting on his corner-stool as if the walk from the changing room had tired him out.

'Any frozen kookaburra specials?' Elvis asked the chip man.

'Talk sense! What you want?' said Olly.

'Half a pound of curry and nineteen chipatis.'

'Do you want to place an order? Or do you want to get out?'

Everybody called him Olly, or Olive Oil. He always looked as if he'd just missed Christmas. He was tall and thin, with a colourless face, and looked like a raw chip with clothes on.

Elvis gave his order.

'Never any variety in here,' he said. 'It'll be better when they open that Indian.'

A place called The Taj Mahal was opening tomorrow in what used to be the chemist's: there was hammering and banging going on in there at all hours of the day.

The fight had just started. Beer-belly had difficulty arising from his stool and it hardly seemed fair because as soon as he managed it Leon knocked him down.

'Beer-belly'll win,' said Elvis.

'Don't talk soft,' said Olly as he wrapped up Elvis's first portion.

'He's gorrit all wrapped up,' said Elvis.

Beer-belly went down for the second time.

'What'd I tell you!' said Olly, almost allowing a smile to creep onto his face.

'He's just having a rest,' said Elvis. 'He's wearing Leon out.'

'You must have cloth between your ears, son!' said Olly.

'He'll batter him to death,' said Elvis as Olly dipped a cod lump in the batter.

Olly glanced at the fight. Beer-belly was looking for the exit now. Leon was posing for the cameras again and trying to work out his next punch.

Olly looked at Elvis as if he was mad.

'Leon's had his chips.' said Elvis as he helped himself to one from the packet Olly was wrapping.

'You don't know what you're on about!'

'Leroy's not worth his salt,' said Elvis as he salted his chips.

'Don't know what they teach you kids at that school nowadays,' said Olly.

'Learnt about square rings today,' said Elvis.

'Eh? What you on about now?'

Elvis waited a minute for Olly to think it out, then gave it up.

They didn't mention Butch and the Gang till they were turning up Chapel Row.

'What for don't you come tomorrow?' Elvis said. 'He won't mind. You know what Butch's like.'

'He can stuff his gang!' said Billy.

'It's your own fault, anyroad.'

'How'd you mek that out?'

'It is.'

'It isn't!'

'Come with me tomorrow, man,' said Elvis when they reached the bottom of Gordon Street. 'Eh? It'll be great!'

'What? Smashing their den to smithereens? I've got better things to do wi' my time.'

'Like what?'

'Like play football,' said Billy.

'Suit yourself,' said Elvis, and he shrugged and walked off.

Chapter 7

But it isn't easy playing football by yourself.

There wasn't a soul about when Billy went down to the rec next morning.

Emma Ward turned up eventually and stood by the slide. He knew what she wanted, so he picked the ball up and went home.

There was nothing on the telly. His mam wanted him to go shopping with her but he said he didn't want to.

Last night his mam had really narked him when his dad was out at the Club. She'd sat out in the kitchen the whole time *The Bobby Downes Spectacular* was on. She refused to watch a second of it. She'd made him feel awful. There'd been this really funny bit. 'What for don't you come in, Mam?' he'd shouted through. 'Because I don't like watching tosh,' she'd answered. Bobby had been playing with his little rubber duck in the bath and dreaming of gorgeous girls, and all the time his wife had been watching his dreams on the telly in the next room, and in the end she flew in and bopped him one with a rolling pin.

After his mam had gone shopping he went up the allotment with his dad, but that was boring.

'Is summat up wi' you, Billy?' his dad asked. 'Summat worrying you?'

'No,' said Billy.

39

He took Dot for a walk along The Edge, but he could see nobody in the quarry or along the Old Line.

When he came back, for some reason his dad told him a daft story about a fireman he'd known called Harry Duggan who had to climb over the yardarm of a ship when he was young and nearly fell off with fright. Boring.

In the afternoon he hung about till his mam said she was sick of him under her feet.

He met Daz coming from the corner shop who started spouting about the raid on the Crag Enders' den.

'They even had a drainpipe for a chimney,' said Daz.

'What did you do with it?'

'Smashed it to smithereens.'

'Great!' said Billy.

'Then we ripped all their floorboards up and chucked them in the marsh.'

'Great!'

'Then we burnt all these old spud sacks they had for curtains.'

'What for?" said Billy.

'For fun.'

'Great!' said Billy.

'It was, Billy. You should've been there. Then Benson turned up.'

'Oh aye?'

'Him and Butch are going to have a fight tomorrow.'

That was something Billy wouldn't mind seeing. Benson was a year older than Butcher and his big brother was a real nut who'd been chucked out of school.

'What time?'

'Two o'clock. Foxcover.'

After tea he hung about. He kept wanting Elvis to call for him.

But when there was a knock on the door it was Joey with his Rasta hat on.

'Want to come round our house, Billy?'

'Don't really fancy it.'

It was what he had been rehearsing saying to Elvis.

'What for?'

'Get yourself out!' Billy's mother shouted.

'There's an interesting picture on tonight,' said Joey 'Howay, man.'

In a way it was all Joey's fault; all that business of the frog had started it.

Billy shook his head.

'Just a pity you can't be friends with somebody sensible like that instead of the stupid Potter lad!' said his mother when Joey had gone.

She wouldn't even let him watch the horror movie when it came on and it was a really good one this time about a giant lettuce with legs coming down from Mars and eating people.

He went to bed early. Maybe things would be better in the morning?

Next morning Billy hung about till he couldn't bear it any longer, then he went round to Elvis's.

The streets were deserted except for little kids and dogs.

He knocked and knocked at the Potters' back door but couldn't make them hear. He could hear them all right, though. Mr Potter and Soss were still arguing about the new people down at the bakery. He let himself in.

The ferrets stared at him from their cage on the kitchen top. Their spiky little eyes reminded him of Mr Brunsdon. The hens were scratting about in their fenced-in bit under the table, where they lived, waiting for some kind soul to shove some crumbs down the hole Mr Potter had bored in the middle to save time and motion.

'I tell you they're not communist!' Soss was saying.

'If they not communists what for they live in a commune – answer me that!'

'Communists don't live in communes, Dad.'

'Don't they? Where do they live, then?'

'Russia.'

'She's mebbies right there, pet,' said Mrs Potter.

'Right me eye!' said Mr Potter.

He and Mrs Potter were sitting on boxes. Soss was standing in front of the mirror, which was the only thing left on the walls. All their pictures of smiling gypsy girls and horses made of exploding fireworks had gone. There wasn't even a carpet on the floor, only the dog, and that was moth-eaten.

'Oh, come in, pet,' said Mrs Potter. 'Have a seat – on the floor! It's all we've got left!' she laughed.

'If they not Russian what for they got all them Ban the Bomb badges on? What for they all got beards if they not Russians?' Mr Potter wanted to know.

'You know what, Dad? You're crackers!'

'I'll gerroff this box and throw it at you in a minute!' said Mr Potter.

'You be careful with your back,' said Mrs Potter. 'Mr Potter's got his back again,' she explained to Billy.

Mr Potter had one of these backs that came and went (a bit like their furniture). It usually came when the Employment Office offered him a job, and usually went when there was a race-meeting.

'You looking for Our Elvis?' Mrs Potter said. 'Want a chocolate, Billy? Sure? Haven't a clue where he is. Want to wait for him? That Cliffy Butcher come in ten minutes ago and they went galloping off like a couple of wild things.'

'He's never in when the coal bucket wants filling!' said Mr Potter.

'Can't you fill it yourself?' asked Soss. 'Or has your bum got stuck to your box?'

'I would do if it wasn't for this back!'

He groaned in agony.

'If you see him tell him we want him to go to The Taj Mahal for our dinners, Billy. Are you off now? Ta-ra.'

'Ta-ra, Mrs Potter.'

He belted up the backs as fast as he could. Just like dozy Daz to get the blinking time wrong! And why hadn't Elvis come round and told him?

At the top of the street Emma Ward was waiting for him.

Typical!

'I'm sick and tired of you following me, Wardy,' he said when he reached her.

'I'm not following you.'

'You are! I'm pig sick of it!'

The words just sprang to his lips. They were out of his mouth before he thought.

She lowered her eyes. He could see she was taken aback. In a way, he wasn't sorry.

'Are you looking for the rest of them?'

'What's it to you?'

'Butch has gone to fight Benson.'

'I know that!'

'Down Foxcover.'

'You don't have to tell me things I already know, Wardy!'

He started for the waste-heap.

'Are you going to watch the fight, Billy?'

He didn't answer her.

'Can I come with you?'

He spun round to face her.

'Look, Wardy, get off my back! I'm not a lass-lad, you know!'

'Nobody said you were.'

'It's all your fault anyroad.'

'What you mean?'

He spun angrily away from her.

Halfway down the path by Rancher Fletcher's he looked up, but she seemed to have gone home.

He belted along the Old Line as fast as he dared. He didn't want to miss seeing Butch get whacked, and he would get whacked. At the same time he didn't want any of the Gang to see him. He didn't want them to know he was still interested.

Well, he wasn't interested, not really.

He didn't give twopence what happened to the Gang. It was just that he would like to see Butch whacked, just for once. It would make a nice change. He'd like to see him humiliated. Love it. He could just imagine Butch crawling.

When he was nearly to Foxcover he heard a shout go up.

That must be Butch getting thumped. A lot of the Crag Enders must have come to see the fight.

He went up the bankside, rolled under the barbed wire and ran across the field as fast as he could.

He went into the top end of Foxcover, where nobody would ever suspect. The shouting was still going on. He pushed his way through the bushes and trees, guided by the noise. They seemed to be close to the Lookout Post that the Crag Enders had wrecked a bit back.

A big shout went up.

Billy pushed aside the branch of a holly bush.

He could see now.

What he saw gave him a shock.

Benson was on the floor. On his hands and knees. There was blood all over his face. Butch was standing above him, swaying a bit but still on his feet.

'Mek him eat muck!' Cloughy shouted.

Butch grinned. He bent down and picked something up off the floor. He started to go towards Benson, a grin on his face.

Billy had seen enough. He shook his head and turned away.

How could anybody support somebody like that? he thought. Is that what they wanted for the leader of their gang? It was pathetic. He didn't want any part of it.

He was across the field and under the wire in no time and before he realised it halfway back along the Old Line, running like mad.

He didn't know why he was running like that.

But he'd be glad when this weekend was over. Things would be better at school.

Chapter 8

But they weren't. They were worse.

For a start off, practically everybody was talking about Butcher's Big Fight. Either that or The Giant Lettuce Picture. Even Soskiss had seen it: her dad was a vegetarian and it was possible he wanted to see the plants getting their own back.

And Butcher joined in the kickabout they always had before the going-in bell went (he usually practised rabbit-punching people this early in the morning) so Billy leaned his back against Miss Benfold's wall and just watched.

Little Chuff came up and started to talk to him. The Gang had found this whistle that didn't work in the marshes, he told Billy, so they'd given it to him.

Billy blew on it hard, nearly popping his ears off, but no sound came.

'The pea's stuck, Chuff,' he said.

'Elvis sez I've swallered it,' said Chuffy, grinning up at him. 'He sez he can 'ear it rattlin' about in me head!'

'Great,' said Billy, handing back the whistle. 'Really useful that, Chuffy – a whistle that doesn't blow.'

Just after that the ball slammed into the wall right above Billy's head. Butcher had mis-kicked again.

Or had he?

Billy was glad when the bell went.

Straight after registration Mrs Drury started boring them silly with the Greeks again.

'They also believed that their heroes, when their life on earth was finished, became immortals and went to live with the gods, among the stars,' she said.

Another load of baloney! Billy thought.

'Now, does anybody know what we call a person who thinks we can read our future in the stars?'

Billy knew. But he wasn't going to say anything.

'An astrologer, miss.'

'Quite right, Samantha.' Samantha Soskiss was the sort of kid that made you puke bucketfuls. She knew everything, *and* a bit extra. 'One house point.'

She wouldn't have given a house point if Billy had answered. If Soskiss didn't win the story prize he'd eat his football boots.

'Of course the gods and spirits were not only in the stars. Everything in nature was inhabited by spirits. Bushes, trees, streams, caves – remember the cave-oracle we talked about last week? Who remembers what an oracle is?'

An oracle was a voice that advised you what to do. Cadmus had consulted the oracle at Delphi and it told him to follow a brindle cow. Sometimes the oracle didn't work, though. Sometimes a wind blew, but no sound came – just like Chuffy's whistle!

'Well done again, Samantha! Another house point. The Greeks even regarded quite ordinary plants as holy.'

('Holy grass!' muttered Elvis, digging Billy in the ribs and nodding down towards the bit of paper Mrs Drury had given them to write study-notes on.)

Billy glanced down and saw that Elvis had drawn a lot of tiddly pinmen bowing down to a giant lettuce and was now adding some lanky stalks of grass. HOLE GRAS he wrote, with an arrow pointing at them.

'Sometimes they would put vine leaves in their hair and go off into the woods, so that they could feel part of nature . . .'

('Which part?' Elvis asked Billy.)

Joey, across the table from Billy, was making notes like mad. He was sacrificing his breaks to finish a mural for the classroom. Michelle Wright was helping him. The pair of them were always going in for competitions on the back of Cornflake packets and winning them for the school.

'Sometimes they drank wine—'

('Yummy-yummy! I like it! I like it!')

'—not to get drunk, of course, the Greeks would never have wanted that—'

('Not much!')

'—but so they could see visions.'

'That's what Our Soss sez, miss,' said Elvis, speaking aloud this time and looking up from his Work of Art. 'Only me dad never believes her.'

Mrs Drury ignored him.

'Then they would go to a sacred grove to worship the wood nymphs and the sacred dryads of the place. A wood – such as Foxcover, for instance – would have been regarded by the Ancient Greeks as sacred.'

She was only saying that about Foxcover because she was getting up a protest to stop it being chopped down to make farming land if the EEC gave Mr Morgan the money. Billy's grandma wouldn't sign her petition because Mrs Drury had got her chucked off the flower-arranging committee at St Luke's.

'Please, miss, we gorra tin box on our mantel shelf in our back kitchen me mam sez is sacred,' said Alison Fretwell.

('Tapped!' said Elvis to Billy, tapping his head with his finger.)

'Really, Alison, dear?'

'Yes, miss, it's what me mam reckons.'

'Why exactly does she say that, dear?'

'The rent-money's in it, miss.'

'I don't quite follow?'

'Miss, me mam sez "Nobody lays a finger on that box because it's sacred!" '

'Ah! I see now! Then nobody touches it?'

'No, miss, me dad goes straight in and gets the money out for the Club, miss.'

A few people laughed, until Mrs Drury glared round at them.

Billy had seen a video round the Potters' where octopuses came down from outer space to shrivel everybody up with these red-hot beams – by coincidence, Mrs Potter burnt the toast while they were watching it – and Mrs Drury had eyes exactly like that, only worse.

'How very interesting, dear,' she said. She glanced round again, burning the last few laughs to a cinder. 'Now, as I was saying a moment ago about Foxcover, every aspect of nature was regarded by the Greeks as holy. Sometimes a mountain was regarded as holy. My own Christian name, for example, is derived from that of a nymph who—'

'Worrizit, miss?'

'I beg your pardon, Butcher?'

'Worrizit, miss?'

'I don't really see that my name has anything to do with this lesson,'

'Go on, miss!'

'Tell us, miss!'

'Please, miss!'

'I'm sorry, I think my Christian name is a personal matter.'

'You know ours, miss.'

'That's different.' Mrs Drury drew herself up to her full height, which was a lot fuller than most folks'. Elvis always said she'd tried twice for the Coldstream Guards but they'd turned her down because she was too big.

'It's Daphne, isn't it, miss?'

That was Patricia Shufflebotham speaking, the big sister of Little Chuff. Between them they knew half of less than nothing (except Mrs Drury's name, possibly?).

'Well really!' said Mrs Drury. 'Is nothing sacred

in this village?'

'Only the Fretwell's rent-money tin, miss,' said Elvis. 'And Foxcover.'

'Whoever asked you to speak, Potter?'

'Thought you asked a question, miss.'

She switched on her Galactic Toaster again. When everybody was well and truly cinderised she said to Pat Shufflebotham:

'Whoever gave you that information, child?'

Pat Shufflebotham didn't reply. She probably couldn't understand. She'd gone all pink.

'Miss, her uncle's a postman,' said Butch. 'He knows everything, miss. And he spreads it round an' all!'

'I don't think that's funny, Butcher!'

('I think it's hilarious, miss!')

'I shall have to speak to the post-mistress about this.'

'Won't do any good, miss,' said Butch.

'Why not?'

'Her uncle's just got the sack.'

'Whatever for?'

('Carry the letters in!')

'He keeps getting this leg, miss.'

'I beg your pardon?'

'He 'as this leg that comes and goes, miss.'

Must be a relation of Mr Potter's back, Billy thought. There was a lot of it about in the village when Billy thought about it. The stomach of the woman who lived next door to Billy's grandma kept coming and going as well. *Mind, my stomach's gone and come back again last night,* she used to say. *Oh dear, Elsie, I am sorry to hear that*, Billy's grandma used to say to her face. Behind her back she said it was all her own fault for being so vain and wearing corsets.

'Is that right, Patricia?'

'Don't know, miss.'

'My dad sez it's because he can sign on the dole again after six months,' said Elaine Partridge.

'That's not a very nice thing to say about anybody, is it?"

'It's true, though, miss.'

To cover her confusion Mrs Drury dived headfirst into the Greek myths again. This story was called Leda and the Swan and was all about another Greek god who disguised himself as a white swan so he could run off with another feller's wife ('Naughty! Naughty!' Elvis kept saying) and when she'd finished Sneck said:

'Please, miss, the feller that lives next door to us did that.'

'Turned himself into a white swan, you mean?' asked Mrs Drury, cracking her Annual Joke.

'No, miss. Ran off with another feller's wife, miss. They ran off to Blackpool.'

'It was Olive Oil's wife, miss,' said Elvis, who had now completed a drawing of a swan with a crown on its head spitting thunderbolts at a lot of pin-men while the HOLE GRAS grass looked on from above, eyes out on stalks. 'At the chippy.'

'I beg your pardon, Potter?'

'He means Mr Hoyle at the fish-and-chip shop, miss,' said Samantha Soskiss, translating.

Billy hadn't known that Mr Hoyle's wife had run away and left him. That was probably why the poor feller always had a face like a long fiddle . . .

Chapter 9

'No, man,' said Elvis when Billy mentioned it in the bogs at break-time. 'It's entirely the other way round.'

'How'd you mean?'

'Remember that time last year when Olly kept laughin' his head off even if you asked him for a bag of free scraps?'

'Aye?'

'*That* was when his wife ran away. Only trouble was, she come back after two weeks. *That's* why Olly never smiles nowadays.'

Elvis zipped up and went out.

Billy took as long as he could to finish off. He wasn't too keen on going out into the yard, especially as Mrs Drury was on duty. She tended to hibernate in the shed, well out of the draught, especially on coldish days, and if trouble broke out between him and Butch she'd probably be the last to hear about it.

Fortunately Butch wasn't in the little yard. Daz shouted for him to join in the football game and passed the ball out to him, but Billy shrugged and pretended he didn't want to play just yet.

Instead, he strolled to the corner of Miss Benfold's classroom so he could poke his nose round into the big yard.

Butch was down at the far end, practising his karate technique with some of the big lads from

55

Mr Fixby's class. No doubt the fact that he'd whupped Tommy Benson had gone to his tiny little head. He probably thought he was champion of the world by now. He really was pathetic.

Billy strolled back to the football game. Elvis had already joined in. For some reason Emma Ward wasn't playing. She was pretending to talk to Deborah Padget. Probably just as well. What did a girl want to play football for, anyhow? They had no real interest in the game. Not really.

But Billy wasn't his usual brilliant self this morning. For some reason he missed a pass that Daz made to him, and a minute later mis-kicked when he had an open goal in front of him.

He knew what was the matter, of course. Butch might be round the corner and out of sight in the big yard, but he wasn't out of Billy's mind. Not by a long chalk. He was practically living in there. Billy couldn't stop thinking about him the last two days.

And, after another couple of errors, when he saw Butch come round Miss Benfold's corner and head towards them, Billy felt almost glad.

Almost.

Butch seemed in joyous spirits. On his way to the football game he rabbit-punched three little kids from Miss Benfold's to the ground who just happened to intercept his flight path. When he reached the game the first thing he did was pick up the tennis ball and kick it deliberately two miles over the wall and into the field that was out of bounds.

'What you want to do that for, man?' asked Daz.

It was the sort of question he shouldn't have asked.

'I'll fetch it!' said Elvis.

He went over the wall like a frog with wings and dropped out of sight.

Butch was slapping Daz around by now, egged-on by Slattery from Fixby's class. He was pretending it was fun, but it wasn't, not all of it.

'You saying I shouldn't have done that?'

'No, man, Butch!'

'You are!'

'I'm not!'

'You contradictin' me?'

'No, man, Butch.'

'You are!'

'I'm not, man!'

'There you go again!'

All the time slap, laugh, slap, laugh. Half in fun, half not.

And Billy knew he was next. This was just warming up for the real thing.

He'd known something like this would happen the moment he saw Mrs Drury putting on her solid leather coat with its lining like four eiderdowns. She'd probably be well into her winter sleep by now, hanging upside-down by her big toes from one of the beams in the shed.

It wasn't funny really.

Billy felt trapped. His back was against the wall. The door to the porch was ten yards to his left. To reach it he'd have to pass Butch. He'd never make it.

'Mek him give you a gee-gee ride, Butch!' said Slattery.

'Turn round,' Butch told Daz.

'What for?'

'Never mind what for!'

Poor Daz. He looked so ashamed as he turned round.

'Bend over!' said Butch. He gave Daz a swift kick up the backside then sprang on his back and dug his heels into his legs. 'Gee-up, cowboy!'

Poor Daz's legs nearly buckled under the weight and for the first few paces he wobbled, but then gradually gained control. Butch made him go round and round in circles. He looked awful.

Why did things like this happen in life? Why did you have to keep going to the dentist's?

The worst of it was, only a tick ago they'd all been playing with Daz, been his friend. Now that was all changed. Nobody dared to say a word to Butch. They were all looking on with sticky smiles on their faces, as if they thought it was all right. Go ahead, Butch, they were all saying. It's OK with us.

Including Billy. The same sticky smile was on his own face. His features seemed to be frozen, wooden, immobile.

He ought to go up to Butch and say, Look, Butch, just pack it up! Just be sensible! But things like that didn't happen in life. Only in pictures, on the telly, in daft books.

And in a minute Butch would be on *his* back. He wouldn't put up a fight. The best thing – the sensible thing – would be to give in, just this time.

He only wished Emma Ward wasn't watching. He knew what would be going through her mind! As if she could do anything about it! Because what

would be the point of putting up a fight against Butch? It would be worse than Leon Leroy against Beer-belly Number Six. Billy had already been on the wrong end of a few of Butch's punches and he could just imagine—

'What the devil's going on here?'

It was Mr Fixby. Nobody liked him, not even the kids in his own class. If he caught you in the porch when you weren't supposed to be there he twisted your arm behind your back. He had hard blue eyes and a jaw like a steam-shovel.

'Nowt, sir, honest. Just a game,' said Butch, already off Daz's back.

'Just a game, eh? I suppose this idiot here volunteered to give you a ride?'

'Yes, sir.'

'Is that correct, Thompson?'

Daz sort of shrugged and gave a wag of his head. It could have meant anything.

'It is true, sir.' said Slattery. 'We all heard him offer, honest to God.'

'It isn't true, Mr Fixby,' said Emma Ward, pushing herself forward. (Deborah Padget trying to hold her back).'Butcher forced him. He's always doing it.'

'Honest to God I never, sir,' said Butcher, 'cross me heart and hope to die!'

'Liar!' Mr Fixby narrowed his eyes as he spoke and his steam-shovel jaw flapped open and shut. No wonder Miss Benfold didn't like him. He was always after her. 'I can only hope you'll show more honesty when you end up in a Court of Law, Butcher – which no doubt you will do one day!'

'How'd you mean, sir?'

'What you've just told me is nothing more than a pack of lies!'

'It isn't lies, sir,' said Butch.

'I swear he's telling the truth, sir.' said Slattery.

'As for you, Slattery, I expect the truth from boys in my class!'

'It is true—'

'You'd swear your mother's life away, Slattery.' The steam-shovel went into top gear now, the eyes were glowing like something hot in a furnace. He was probably doing it on purpose to try and look hard. 'The whole lot is a pack of lies. I know that because I observed the whole incident from that window up there.'

He pointed up at the window in Miss Benfold's. Miss Benfold was peering down. She was small and neat and had black hair that always looked tidy. Emma Ward was her favourite pupil, because she was so good at gym and all that. Emma Ward was always trying to model herself on Miss Benfold.

Or used to. Billy noticed she'd done something funny to her hair and was already beginning to look like gormless Deborah Padget who hung around corner ends every night trying to get off with lads.

'I saw every sordid little rotten detail!' the steam-shovel said. 'You're nothing but a bully, lad!'

'That's not true, sir,' said Butch.

'I beg your pardon, lad!'

'Just a bit of fun, that's all.'

'You might think so, but other folks might not! I think you'd better go to Mr Starr's office at dinnertime. Would you like that?'

'Don't mind, sir.'

It wasn't exactly a treat to be sent to Mr Starr's office: but Butch had been plenty of times before.

'In that case, perhaps you wouldn't mind missing the football practice as well?'

Butch shrugged his shoulders and looked down.

'Not so fond of that, I see! In that case I'll speak to Miss Benfold and personally see to it that you miss the next two football practices! All right?'

'If you like, sir.'

'I don't like your tone, lad! What exactly do you mean by that?'

Mr Fixby came right over and jammed his ugly mug right up against Butch's.

'What I say, sir. It's up to you.'

Mr Fixby was looking really mad now.

'I'll tell you what I'll do, lad. I hear you're being considered for the team against Middleham? I shall see to it personally that your name is scrubbed off the list. All right? Personally! Okay? Got the message?'

'Please, sir!' said Emma.

Mr Fixby ignored her.

'All right, Butcher?'

'Yes, sir.'

'And after you've seen Mr Starr you can get to my room immediately! I'd like a little chat session with you – if you don't mind!'

'Please sir!' Emma said again.

But he didn't seem to hear her as he stalked after Butch through the porch door.

'What you trying to do, Wardy? Drop him further in it?' asked Cloughy.

'No, I was—'

But nobody was listening to her.

Elvis came back over the wall with the ball.

'Pigsby for king!' he shouted. 'They should bring back hanging for fellers like him!' he rolled the ball towards Billy.

But Billy completely missed it.

Chapter 10

That was the last time Billy had a kickabout in the yard for practically yonks.

He did have a game that dinnertime. But that was only for five minutes. Until Mr Starr let Butch out. Pity, really, because Billy had been really on form. With Daz as a partner he'd scored three goals.

Butch barged out of the back-porch door like one on those bulls you see let out into the bullring in Spain. Exactly like that. Head down, horns twitching.

Oh boy! thought Billy.

'What happened?' Daz asked Butch.

'Sez I won't be in the team against Middleham,' said Butch.

'That's not fair,' said Daz.

'Meks no odds to me,' said Butch. 'Let's get the ball away!'

He glared at Emma, but once he started playing he seemed good-humoured. Till Billy got the ball. Then he started barging in from the back and all that. He did it every time.

So Billy packed up after two or three times. He couldn't see the point of trying to play when there were idiots like that around.

'What's up, Chicken?' Butch called after him as Billy walked away. Billy didn't answer.

He knew what was going on, of course. All

Butch wanted was a fight – especially after whacking Benson. That was the way his tiny little mind worked. It was the *only* way it worked.

Even when Billy dropped out of the kickabouts Butch still couldn't let him alone. From then on he kept nudging him as he went past. Tapping him. Calling him names. It was pathetic.

Mr Starr noticed sharp enough when Billy stopped playing football in the yard. How he knew these things, Billy hadn't a clue, because he hardly budged out of his office and the windows looked into the big yard and the shed anyhow.

'Anything wrong?' he asked when he called Billy in, Wednesday afternoon break.

'How'd you mean, sir?'

'I've noticed you haven't been playing football lately, that's all.'

'Just don't fancy it, sir.'

Mr Starr looked at him. He was an ancient man. It was funny to think that years ago he had played for the Athletic when they'd won the FA cup.

'I don't like the sound of that. I like my stars to keep in training, you know.' He didn't smile when he said that. Didn't make a joke of it. 'You haven't forgotten the Middleham match next week?'

'No, sir.'

'You know Miss Benfold would like to try you out for captain? I think it'll be useful practice for you. Think you can manage?'

'Sir.'

Mr Starr looked at him.

'Nothing wrong, is there?'

'No, sir.'

'You seem a bit tense, that's all. There's no need to worry. A lot of the team will be lads your own age, anyhow. Miss Benfold tells me you suggested putting Emma Ward in the team?'

Billy nodded. He hesitated just before he nodded, though. And the hesitation seemed to tell Mr Starr just as much as the nod.

'Not so fond of that idea now?' Mr Starr paused to give a chance for Billy to reply, then went on: 'Myself, I thought it was an excellent suggestion. Something happened to change your mind?'

'No, sir.'

'Ah well.' Another pause. 'And then there's the real problem. What about Clifford Butcher?'

Billy's heart leapt into his mouth when Mr Starr said that name. He felt himself go red. Did Mr Starr know all about him and Butcher? How could he?

'You know Mr Fixby wants him left out of the team? Apparently Butcher was very rude to him the other day in the yard, I gather you saw it?'

'Sir.'

'And what do you think? Point is, I know up to now you've always been a striker, but if you are going to be captain next year I'd prefer you at midfield defence – what we used to call centre half in the old days. I think that's the right place for a captain. What do you think?'

'Sir.'

'Not too sure?"

'I can tackle and all that, sir,' said Billy.

'I'm sure you can, Billy. So that leaves us needing a striker. Obvious choice is to push

Tommy Bellwood forward, but it might give Middleham Middle a bit of heart if we leave him out this time!' He chuckled and winked. Tommy Bellwood, the school captain, had scored three goals last time. 'I was thinking of playing Clifford Butcher, he's the obvious choice, but now that this business with Mr Fixby has cropped up, we might have to think of somebody else. Any ideas?'

'There's Daz Thompson, sir.'

'Darrell's all right. He has some fancy tricks. But has he as much punch as Butcher? A striker needs a bit of go about him. Could he do it, do you think?'

Billy shrugged.

He didn't say anything, but he was thinking "punch" is the right word as far as Butcher is concerned!

'Ah, well, nothing's decided yet. We'll see about it. And you get some practice in, young man – you hear me? You know Miss Benfold can't hold her usual football practice this week because of this action the teachers are involved in?'

'Sir.'

'Get yourself down to the rec, you hear me?'

'Oh, I will, sir,' said Billy, nodding his head and looking eager.

But even as he spoke he knew he wouldn't.

He'd gone down the rec on Tuesday night, half-intending to play if Butch wasn't there throwing his weight about. As it happened, he wasn't. But the rest of them were all talking about Butch. Benson's big brother was after him, apparently. Butch said he didn't care. Big head! Benson's big brother had been chucked out of the comprehensive because the teachers couldn't handle him and he'd sprayed some stuff in a kid's face. The rest of them seemed to think Butch was some sort of hero or something. Even Joey.

Billy had pretended he was running a message and went straight past.

At school he hung about the yard, pretending to talk to lads he didn't like, pretending to laugh at jokes he'd heard before.

All the time there was only one thought in his mind: *Keep out of that idiot's way!*

It was daft, really, spending your whole playtime doing that. But the more he thought about Butch the more he made him puke nowadays. He was such a bragger, such a bombhead, such a freak!

Not that the rest of them were any better. Tuesday dinnertime he went in to help Joey and Michelle Wright with the mural. He thought he might as well.

Joey had some great ideas, he could see that. Like making their den the scene for the cave oracle, a spooky misty object at the back of the tunnel that you couldn't quite see, and turning Foxcover into a Sacred Grove.

And Billy enjoyed helping, at least for five minutes. After that he kept hearing the roar from the yard outside – a bit like the roar of the fair that came every year about autumn – and wanting to be out there again, where it was all happening, instead of cutting out swords that Joey had drawn for him.

But when he was out there in the yard he didn't do anything. Just hung around. He didn't seem to be able to join in. He didn't even want to.

And what really narked was that the others didn't seem to notice anything was wrong. Elvis, Daz, Bozzy – that lot. They all seemed as happy as Larry.

Wednesday night he went round to call for Elvis and stopped just in time as he was crossing their yard; Butch was in their back kitchen, playing with the ferrets.

So he went round to Daz's instead.

And played a boring game for half-an-hour with questions about capital cities and stuff like that. It was the sort of game Daz liked.

Daz told him Benson's brother was supposed to be really after Butch now because Butch had said he was a plonker.

'What *is* a plonker, anyroad?' asked Billy.

'Haven't a clue,' said Daz, 'but the capital city of the USA is Washington,' he said, 'and that's three more points to me.'

'Serves him right,' said Billy. 'He should never have made Benson eat dirt.'

'When did he do that?'

'Sunday morning, man, up at Foxcover.'

'I never saw him do that.'

'You can't have been looking very hard!'

'Mebbies I wasn't,' laughed Daz. He never noticed these things. He drew a card and said, 'What was Ringo Starr's real name?'

Billy hated these games.

'Richard Starkey,' said Daz. 'Two points!'

And Billy hated being fenced-in like he was being. Or was it shut out? Because it wasn't only in the school yard and down at the rec. It was in the streets, the quarry, the Old Line, all over . . .

Something was happening. A wall was going up round him. It wasn't his fault, it was theirs, all of them. Well, Butcher's, really.

He'd laid the first rotten brick that afternoon in the den last weekend. It was him to blame.

It wasn't fair.

'Capital of Sweden?' asked Daz.

'Hong Kong?' said Billy.

On Thursday afternoon he didn't even bother to wait for Elvis or Daz or Joey or anybody, but ran all the way home by himself.

He told himself as he belted along Station Road and past Chapel Row and then up Wolsely that it was all part of the training he'd promised to do for Mr Starr.

But that wasn't the real reason why he ran.

Chapter 11

The Arab was on the news again that night. His men were falling back under heavy bombardment. He said it was a set-back, but not a defeat.

'One day we shall return to our homelands,' he said, smiling. Mortar bombs were flying round his ears: even as he spoke a whole wall collapsed and further down the street a woman screamed.

'Beats me what they're fighting for!' said Billy's dad. 'Nowt but sand when it's all there!'

He was right. Mrs Drury had told them how the whole Mediterranean was once lush with trees and jungle, elephants in it and everything, but the goats had gone about deliberately chewing the bark off every little bush and tree and eventually turned it into a desert.

That sounded a bit far-fetched, but she might just be on the right track for once, because Billy had definitely seen Rancher Fletcher's goats chewing the bark off bushes up the Old Line and he'd even seen one eating an old pair of size eleven pit boots that Elvis had pulled out of somebody's dustbin and worn down to the den just to give everybody a giggle. Goats probably ate anything. They might even eat Butcher if they were offered the chance!

After the adverts it was *Looking Out*, the local news programme.

'It's on lass!' Billy's dad shouted. 'Are you coming to see Matty?'

'I've got better things to do with my time than gawp at Matty Brunsdon!' Billy's mam shouted back from the kitchen.

'Good evening, all you good people out there,' said the presenter, Lord La-de-dah, smiling and displaying his prize gnashers. He had the sort of teeth that were normally reserved for adverts. Grandma and Billy's mam were always having arguments about whether they were false or not. 'Tonight, viewers, we have a very full programme indeed, and later on we shall be going down on the farm to interview Minnie the Only Talking Duck in Our Beloved Northlands – would you believe!'

'We'd believe owt of this programme, lad!' said Billy's dad.

'But first,' said Lord La-de-dah's co-presenter, 'we have an up-to-date report on the growing trouble at the Belton Buildings Industrial Estate.'

The co-presenter's name was Valerie Figg and Billy's grandma called her a nobody because her Aunty Ida lived down Wolsely Street and her Uncle Wally had only one leg because the other was run over by a steam-roller under the viaducts during the war. Everybody called him Lucky Figg, probably because the steam-roller hadn't run his other leg over as well.

'Howay in, lass!' shouted Billy's dad.

Billy's mam didn't answer.

Mr Brunsdon was sitting in a tubular steel

chair and for the first five minutes he behaved almost like a normal civilised human being.

But when Mr Chatterington-Bumleigh, the representative of the big multinational that owned the factory where Billy's dad worked, mentioned that some men had been sent to cause trouble at their factories in Wales, Mr Brunsdon started rocking back and forth like this poor feller Billy had seen in a horror movie round at Elvis's where a mad professor kept giving him electric shocks to improve his brain.

'Hold on there! Steady on!' he kept saying, interrupting all the time.

'Indeed, I would go as far as to say that one man was deliberately chosen to spearhead the trouble in our Welsh workforce,' said Mr Chatterington-Bumleigh.

'That'll be Tommy Butcher!' said Billy's dad, reaching for his pipe.

'Who do you mean by that?' demanded by Mr Brunsdon.

'I am not in a position to name names – but this man is well-known as a hooligan and trouble-maker.'

'I told you!' Billy's dad exclaimed. 'I knew it was Tommy Butcher!'

'I'm not going to stand here and listen to this twaddle!' shouted Mr Brunsdon, who was still sitting down.

'Now, now,' said La-de-dah, 'this is hardly fair to Mr Chatterington-Bumleigh here.'

'Fair? Fair! Who's talking about fair?' The

tubular steel chair took a real battering this time. 'What's fair about this feller over there to begin with?'

Mr Brunsdon pointed his prize sausage finger at Mr Chatterington-Bumleigh. Billy could see why Mr Brunsdon had been called The Belton Brute in his wrestling days. He was once supposed to have thrown a man clean out of the ring at West Hartlepool and break his neck and then laugh about it while folks threw beer bottles at his head. But other folks said he used to break the same feller's neck every night for weeks and that it was all a put-up job and they split the money on the empties between them.

'If he had one iota of fairness about him he'd get hisself out of this country and back to where he comes from in the first place!'

'But I come from Surbiton!'

'Never heard of it! Where's that?'

'This is absurd!'

'Is it your intention to shut this factory down – or not?'

'Absolute nonsense!' replied Mr Chatterington-Bumleigh.

'Don't call me nonsense, mister!' said Mr Brunsdon.

'There's gonna be trouble!' said Billy's dad, lighting up his pipe. 'Sure as shot there's going to be trouble!'

'You sound pleased about it!' said Billy's mam, who had come to the doorway.

'Don't be soft, woman!'

'This whole interview is becoming ridiculous,'

said Mr Chatterington-Bumleigh, adjusting his tie.

'Oh! I'm ridiculous now, am I—'

'Nobody—'

'I'll tell you what's ridiculous, Mr Chatterbox – or whatever you're name is—'

'That's it, Matty, lad!' said Billy's dad, blowing out a cloud of smoke that wrapped itself round the telly.

'It's ridiculous that this government's given you lot a grant amounting to thousands of millions of pounds—'

'Ridiculous!'

'—and now that you've sucked all the perks dry you want to up-stumps and off somewhere else where the grass is greener on the other side of the river back where you came from!'

'That's telling them straight, Matty, lad!'

'SURBITON! SURBITON! I COME FROM SURBITON!'

'So you can put that in your Surbiton big pipe and smoke it!' said The Belton Brute.

'Right, Matty, lad!' said Billy's dad.

'Now, now, we must keep calm,' said La-de-dah, who by now was looking anything but. His face had gone a pale shade of green. 'If we could let Mr Chatterington-Bumleigh finish,' he said.

For a few seconds Mr Brunsdon restrained himself, but as Mr Chatterington-Bumleigh drew to a close he began fidgeting on his poor chair, as if eager for the bell to go for Round Two.

'And, finally, what we have all to bear in mind here,' said Mr Chatterington-Bumleigh, 'is that we are in the throes of a world situation. My company – Krapp Ringhorn Spitz – like all companies, must compete to stay alive. That's what life is all about, and if my good friend over there—'

That was it! A bell must have sounded in Mr Brunsdon's head.

With one fell swoop The Belton Brute bounded out of his corner.

'GOOD FRIEND!' he bellowed, 'GOOD FRIEND!'

'Seconds out of the ring!' shouted Billy's dad, and his pipe fell out of his mouth, 'Watch this bit, lass!' And he plugged his pipe back into his mouth.

'I'm no GOOD FRIEND of yours, mister! I'll have you know I'm choosy about the company I keep! So don't start GOOD FRIENDING me because you're on the wrong side of this horse by a long chalk!'

'Absurd!' said Mr Chatterington-Bumleigh.

Billy saw that La-de-dah now seemed to be concealing himself behind a conveniently placed green studio plant.

'Who you calling names?' asked The Brute, waddling forward, legs straddled like one of those Japanese wrestlers that grandma always called satsumas, to claim the centre of the ring. 'Are you looking for a knuckle sandwich, mister, like?'

He took a step forward and stumbled. He must

have caught his foot in a wire. Something banged
off camera and two pops sounded as bulbs
exploded. Mr Brunsdon went down with a crash
that must have woken up every satsuma wrestler
having forty winks in far-off Japan.

'You laughing at me, mister?'

'Certainly not!' whinnied Mr Chatterington-
Bumleigh.

'YOU ARE! I'M NOT GOING TO TAKE THIS
LYING DOWN!' shouted Mr Brunsdon, who by
now had regained his feet.

Mr Brunsdon swung a wild punch. There was a
shriek. The picture wobbled and swung, then
something flew across the studio: it *could* have
been La-de-dah's teeth. It could have been Mr
Chatterington-Bumleigh's. Or even Mr Brunsdon's. There was a definite clacking sound. And
the screen went black.

'Good lad, Matty! Good lad!' shouted Billy's dad,
groping for his pipe which had headed for cover
down the side of the chair he was sitting on.

Soft music began to play. A card made a nervous
jerky entrance with the words: NORMAL
SERVICE WILL BE RESUMED AS SOON AS
POSSIBLE.

'That'll mek a change!' laughed Billy's dad.

'I thought you were the one that was against
violence?' said Billy's mam just behind them.

'Don't be daft, woman! This isn't violence. This
is different. That feller deserves all he got. And
you have to laugh at Matty Brunsdon.'

'Maybe you don't take him seriously enough,
Dick,' said Billy's mother. 'And, by the way,

78

what's all them bits of boards and post a feller's just dumped in our yard?'

'Oh, them's for picket signs Matty asked us to knock together for him.'

'Not in our house,' she said. 'You hear me?'

Chapter 12

On Friday morning Billy was talking to a lad called Fenton – who he didn't normally care twopence about – when out of the corner of his eye he saw Butch coming towards him, Slattery tagging along behind, a stupid grin on both their faces.

This is blinking it! he thought.

He felt certain Butch was going to challenge him to a fight. Slattery had probably put him up to it. It would be a daft thing to do in the playground, a stupid thing. But then Butch *was* stupid.

Billy pretended not to notice him coming. He kept on looking at Fenton, pretending to listen to what he was saying, though he hadn't a clue what the words were. His heart started racing, his throat went dry in a second and his tongue seemed to be stuck to the top of his mouth. The worst thing was Emma Ward wasn't two yards away and watching. For some reason she always was!

But, in fact, all Butch said was:

'Don't want you in Foxcover any more, Robinson.'

Billy didn't say anything. He was completely taken aback. He hadn't expected this. He looked blankly at Butch.

'Got that?' Butch asked.

'Never again!' giggled Slattery.

'Don't want to go in Foxcover anyhow,' said Billy.

'Just as well!' said Butch. 'Because you're not allowed to!'

He did his stupid eyeball act, glowering down at Billy, Slattery sniggering behind him, then swaggered off.

Billy felt pretty chuffed at first.

His voice hadn't shaken too much – hardly at all – when he answered Butch. And what he'd said was pretty cheeky, really, when you thought about it: *Don't want to go in Foxcover anyhow*. In other words, You can stuff Foxcover, Butcher! And after Butch had finished he had almost said: Big deal! He would have said it if Butch hadn't suddenly walked away. He'd stayed pretty cool. He hoped Wardy had noticed that. He knew she thought he was scared of Butcher. He could see that in her eyes. They all thought he was scared. They were all wrong!

It was only afterwards that Billy began to have second thoughts.

What the heck right had Butch anyway to tell him to stop away from Foxcover, anyhow? None. It would soon be the EEC's, in any case, unless Drury's daft campaign succeeded, and then where would Butcher be? All the trees would be chopped down. There would just be a field full of nowt. Who cared!

And, anyhow, what right had Butcher to order him about, in the first place? He should have told him where to get off there and then. He should have said something like: *Look, Butcher, in the*

*first place you don't own Foxcover, right? In the
second place you don't order me around because
I'm not in your stupid gang any more, and I don't
take orders from anybody – especially you!*

That's what he should have said to him. That
would have made Butcher sit up. He could just
imagine the look on his silly face. He could just
imagine the look on Emma Ward's as well.

Trouble was, he could never think of the right
words to say when he was caught on the hop like
that. They always occurred to him five minutes
too late!

At dinnertime he didn't go out in the yard. By
standing on the hot water pipe in the bogs he could
see out of the window into the yard and the first
thing he saw was Slattery and Butcher ranging
about looking for somebody – obviously him – so
Billy ran back up the corridor and into Mrs
Drury's.

Joey and Michelle Wright had nearly finished
the mural now. On the wall above the fish tank
they were doing the bit where the warriors who
had sprung from the dragon's teeth had killed
themselves, until only five remained, the five that
Cadmus was going to use to build his new city.

'Brilliant, eh?' said Joey.

Michelle just smiled. She was a shy girl who
never said anything. She always had plenty to say
to Joey, though.

'Seen worse,' said Billy.

In fact Joey was a pretty good artist. Cadmus
and the five warriors were standing in Foxcover.
Billy could recognise the Lookout Post and a holly

bush that was all fat and comfy like a tea cosy. Joey had even put in the big tree with the magpie's nest that nobody ever managed to climb up to yet.

Then he noticed a funny thing. A face – it had a slight look of Billy about it – was looking out from the ring of bushes round the sort of circle where the fight had been. Just a face. As if somebody was sneaking a look.

That was OK. Trouble was, one of the soldiers had exactly the same face as the guy peeping out. That wasn't like Joey. He usually didn't make mistakes, not in art.

'It isn't a mistake,' Joey said, smiling and looking at Michelle, who seemed to be in on the joke.

'But they're the same feller,' said Billy.

'It was this idea Joey had,' said Michelle.

'Real brill!' said Joey.

'How'd you mean?'

'Like you could have this feller who sort of wanted to be in two places at once. Couldn't make up his mind. Get it?'

Billy pretended he got it, though he hadn't. Not really.

He passed twenty minutes away cutting out leaves (it was all they'd let him do) while Joey put the finishing touches to Cadmus's face.

Unfortunately, he was making him look a bit like Butch. Same stupid big jaw. Same way of standing. He even seemed to be eyeballing the five survivors!

Naturally, Billy's leaves didn't satisfy Joey.

Too spiky, he said. Joey was that fussy, he was like an old woman sometimes. It was only a daft mural when it was all there!

Billy was quite glad when Miss Benfold popped her head round the door and caught him. She was on duty, carrying a cup of tea.

'Who gave you permission to be in here, Billy Robinson?'

'He's helping us, miss,' said Joey.

'Is he really, Michelangelo? Do you think I could possibly have a word with him outside in the corridor?'

Billy thought she was going to chuck him out in the yard, but it wasn't that.

'You're all right for the game next Tuesday?'

'Yes, miss.'

'I've noticed you're not playing football in the yard nowadays. You're not injured?'

'No, miss.'

'So you'll be all right for captain?'

Billy blushed and nodded.

'I've spoken to Tommy Bellwood, and he thinks it's a good idea if he stands down this once to give you the practice. That's nice of him, isn't it?'

'Yes, miss.'

'One other thing. Emma. Do you still think it's a good idea to put her in the team?'

Billy hesitated.

'Having second thoughts? Well I thought it was a good idea, Billy. I thought it was very – brave of you, really – to suggest it in the first place. So we'll give her a go, shall we?'

'If you like, miss.'

'You seem lukewarm. Nothing happened, has there?'

'No, miss.'

She looked down at him for a moment.

'We don't want to lose on Tuesday, Billy. We don't want to slaughter them like we did last time. But you know how Mr Starr feels about losing. One other thing. Emma has been to see me. She thinks Cliffy Butcher should be allowed to play after all, in spite of what happened in the yard the other day, which I must say is pretty big of her. What do you think? Mr Starr tells me you suggested playing Darrell Thompson instead.'

'Yes, miss.'

'If we do push you back into defence we'll need somebody up front who can score goals.'

'Daz's pretty nifty, miss.'

'Nifty, yes. But will he score goals, Billy? Leave this one with me, will you? I'll see if I can squeeze Darrell in somewhere.'

'OK, miss.'

'And get some training in yourself, will you?'

'Yes, miss.'

He didn't, though, not that day. Not really.

He swanned about in the yard all afternoon break.

He ran all the way home again – you could count that as training if you liked.

He did go down to the rec after tea, but Butch was there lolloping about like an idiot, showing off, always going to his right, of course. Billy guessed by the way he was shouting his head off that Miss Benfold had told him he was going to be in the team.

After watching this display through the railings for a minute Billy sneaked away.

He went up to the top of Wolsely and practised his swerving banana and bendy shots against the wall for ten minutes. But it was boring, playing football all by yourself, and eventually the feller from the top house came out and gave him a telling-off for waking him up.

It was nearly as bad when he went home.

As soon as he went in the kitchen he knew something was up. It wasn't only that his dad was home already (his work boots and overalls were dumped just inside the back door where he always stepped out of them when he came home and left them for his mother to tidy away, which she hadn't done this time).

'They've come out on strike, pet.' Billy's mam said, when he asked her. '*Unofficial!*'

'What difference does that make, woman?' asked Billy's dad as he padded back into the kitchen in his stockinged feet. 'Them down London know nowt!'

Billy's mam made her camel noise and handed him his toasted teacake and his pot of tea.

'And what do you intend doing now?'

'I've told Matty I'll do first picket.'

'Picket! Picket! That's all you think about!'

'He's coming for us at half-past to take us up in his car.'

'*His* car? You mean the union's car, don't you? Can't you see that? You and the rest of the silly fools have paid for that. It's a pity we won't have a car any more!' She meant that if they were on strike Billy's dad wouldn't have the use of the factory van any more to go shopping, like they did sometimes. It was better than waiting three weeks for the bus and then getting told off for not having the right change. And they wouldn't be able to use it to go down to Barnsley to see Sandra and Steven and Little Julie. 'And what about all them sticks and boards still cluttering up my yard out there?'

'We're taking them with us.'

'Good!'

'Up to your mother's. Matty's had a word with her this afternoon and she's going to lend us a bit of a hand.'

'Matty Brunsdon'll use anybody to further his own cause!'

'Don't get aerated, Alice. You know what your mother's like, she likes a fight, mebbies she wants to help.'

A car horn sounded outside their back yard.

'I'll come with you, if you like, Dad,' said Billy.

They both seemed surprised.

'Don't you want to go out and play?' his mother said. 'And I thought you told me you had another story to write?'

'Thought I'd do that Sunday night.'

'I'll tek you up tomorrow morning, son.' his dad said. 'That's when your grandma and Mr Wainwright's gonna make a start. All right? Back in time for supper, lass,' he said to Billy's mam.

'What supper? You're getting no supper here. I'm going on strike and all!'

Mr Brunsdon lumbered through the back yard gate and began to gather up the picket things.

'We'll see about that when we come back, lass,' said Billy's dad. 'Do you think I want to go on strike, lass? We all have to stick together at a time like this, haven't we? Eh? What other chance have we got? Give us a kiss and I'll be off.'

Chapter 13

Grandma was singing:

> *Fight the good fight,*
> *With all thy might,*
> *God is thy strength*
> *And Christ thy right.*

She was a very keen church-goer. She never missed. She went every Sunday and always wore her white gloves because she wanted to make absolutely sure of a place in heaven.

Grandad was already up there, keeping the seat warm for her, as she used to say. He'd been up there a few years now, since before Billy had been born, though he was sometimes allowed down here on a weekend pass to give her a cuddle in bed.

So she said. She was a real big fibber.

She was cutting out squares of card to paste on the boards of the picket signs. Mr Wainwright, Grandma's fancy man, was nailing the boards to the stakes on the concrete path outside her back door.

'Do you think you should always forgive your enemies, Grandma?'

'Always, pet. It's what the Bible sez: *Fear the Lord and forgive your enemies.*'

'Did you forgive Hitler, Grandma?'

'I couldn't, pet. Not after what he did to your Uncle Ronnie.'

'What did he do, Grandma?'

'Shot him down in his aeroplane.'

Until he was quite old Billy thought that Hitler had personally climbed into an aeroplane and shot Uncle Ronnie down out of pure spite over the English Channel, but that turned out to be not the case. As far as Billy could make out Hitler was too old and doddery to fight by the time he started the war, and he'd hired other fellers to fight his battles for him.

Uncle Ronnie's photo stood on Grandma's sideboard, between the clock that never went (which had belonged to grandma's Aunt Nora) and the silver-plated lady with no clothes on holding a flower-holder.

Funny thing was, although he was only a photograph now, you always thought of him as a person. He was always there, listening in to what was going on, like one of the family. When you played cards he watched you. And, sometimes, when the firelight flickered over his face you could see him nodding, as if to say *I don't want you cheating, Our Billy!*

It was his uncle's Air Force hat that had reminded Billy of Princess Di's the other night. He'd realised that the moment he came into Grandma's room. *Fancy you forgetting that!* Uncle Ronnie seemed to say to him.

It was a funny thing that Princess Di should be wearing the same kind of hat to open a school that Uncle Ronnie had been killed in.

'Do you think it's right to fight, Grandma?'

'Love your neighbour is what the Bible says.'

'What did you fight the war for then?'

'The war was different, pet. Hitler was getting over-big for his boots and somebody had to put him in his place. He thought he could do what he liked with the British. He kept grabbing one country after another. Poland and somewhere else. So somebody had to show him what's what.'

'Didn't God mind?'

'How could He, pet? God was on our side. He always has been.'

'Did God tell you that?'

'Not in so many words, Billy. But we all knew in our hearts, didn't we Tommy?'

'Aye,' said Mr Wainwright who had just come in for a breather, 'if you say so, lass.'

Mr Wainwright had never so much as seen the inside of a church. He'd told Billy that himself. 'Never once blackened the doorstep of a church since I was married, Billy,' he had said, 'and shan't do again till they carry us away in me little wooden box. Though once,' he had added, 'when I was trapped in a roof-fall down the pit I have to admit I got down on me knees and prayed to God to come and get us out sharp.' 'And did he?' Billy had asked. 'Depends what way you want to look at it, son,' Mr Wainwright had answered. 'All I know is it was your grandad and two deputies that pulled me out alive.'

Mr Wainwright had his own funny ideas about God. Once when they were out for a walk he'd lifted Billy up to look at a blackbird's nest. 'See

that?' he asked Billy. 'That's God in there, Billy.'
Billy had looked and looked for ages but all he
could see was five greenish eggs. At first he
thought that maybe Mr Wainwright had made a
mistake because God was that big he couldn't
possibly get in a bird's nest. A bit after that it had
occurred to him that maybe he'd been looking for
the wrong thing and that God was really so tiny
he hadn't noticed him among the eggs. Then, a bit
later, it occurred to him that wasn't what Mr
Wainwright was talking about at all. You
gradually realised these things as you got older.

Was Grandad in the war?' Billy asked.

'He wanted to be, pet, but they wouldn't let him.
The government said they couldn't spare him
from the pits. He was one of the best coal-hewers
in existence in them days – wasn't he, Tommy?'

'Next to me,' said Mr Wainwright.

'And would he have liked this strike?'

'Certainly. I know that for a definite fact,'

'Has he been down to see you again?'

'He popped down for ten minutes last night.'
Mr Wainwright coughed.

'And what did he say?'

' "Fight the good fight, with all thy might, lass,"
he told me.'

Mr Wainwright coughed again.

Billy's dad said his grandma was a bigger liar
than Tommy Pepper. Billy wasn't sure who
Tommy Pepper was, but if he was anything like
his grandma he must have been a heck of a liar.

'Was Grandad ever on strike, Grandma?' Billy
asked.

'I sometimes used to think he was never off it, pet. Just after we were married there was a really big strike. All the men came out. We lived on bread-and-dripping for weeks. We used to walk about in the dark because we couldn't afford the lights on. A man down Hope Street ate his own boots to stay alive.'

Mr Wainwright nearly coughed his tonsils up.

'What's the matter with you? It's the barefaced truth I'm telling him!'

'Who said it wasn't, lass?' said Mr Wainwright.

Billy poured himself another glass of lemonade then screwed the top back on the pop bottle and set it up on the table.

'What happened in the strike, Grandma?'

'Everybody used to troop down to Foxcover—the weather was champion. A swig of pop and a crust of bread used to last us all day. The men ran runny-races along the Old Line and played football in the fields till the bobbies came and stopped them.'

'What did they stop them for, Grandma?'

'Because they were enjoying themselves, pet.'

'But what did you go down to Foxcover for?'

'It was the best place to be, pet. There was nothing to do in the house. We took jam-and-bread sandwiches. The bairns gathered flowers and the women sat and talked. Your Uncle Ronnie gathered that many bluebells we had to stand them in buckets in the back yard. Everybody was fond of Foxcover. Especially him over there!' she said nodding at Mr Wainwright.

'Aye!' said Mr Wainwright, winking.

'How's that?' asked Billy.

'It was where he did his courting,' said Grandma, nudging Billy in the ribs.

'And you two, woman! The pair of you were never out of there.'

'Never in the wide world!'

Grandma made a bite to eat at dinnertime, and after that Mr Wainwright had his pipe and then fell asleep in front of the fire. He made a hubble-bubble noise when he snored, like Billy's sister's coffee percolator.

'He can't keep awake nowadays,' said Grandma as she sipped her coffee in her rocking chair by the fire.

'Is he older than you, Grandma?'

'Not quite, pet, but he's had a hard life.'

'How do you mean?'

'Tommy's never been the same since he lost his wife. They loved one another.'

Mr Wainwright hubble-bubbled. It seemed funny to think of somebody who made a noise like that being in love with somebody.

'He ought to be reported to the council,' said Grandma. 'They call it Noise Pollution nowadays.' She took another sip. She was always that lady-like. Billy's mam held her cup in exactly the same way, with her little finger stuck up in the air like that. 'He was always fighting on when he was a lad.'

'Mr Wainwright?'

He was such a little feller, and gentle. He always wore a rose in his buttonhole, wrapped with silver paper, and always gave it to Grandma soon as he came in.

'Fought like a banty-cock when he was young, pet. Never stopped. Went off like a firecracker if anybody opened their mouth to him in them days. Laid many a big feller out.'

She put her cup down on the fireplace tiles, and in five minutes *she* was asleep as well.

What a funny thing life was, Billy thought. He couldn't imagine Mr Wainwright laying fellers out.

Hubble-bubble

And Uncle Ronnie, dead all those years. Billy wondered how old he was when he had been shot down. He didn't look very old. It was funny how being killed had made him look young forever.

He seemed to be staring out at Billy, looking straight into his eyes, as if trying to tell him something.

Billy stood up, quietly, so that The Sleeping Beauties wouldn't hear, and went to the sideboard.

What you trying to tell me? he asked Uncle Ronnie. Not aloud, of course. Ghosts didn't need words. What are you trying to say?

But Uncle Ronnie didn't answer, not then. He just smiled out at Billy, as if to say *Wait and see* . . .

Billy went into Grandma's kitchen. Although it was early afternoon a car going along Churchfield Road had its lights blazing. The whole afternoon was dripping with fog. The trees had hardly any leaves, though they were covered in buds. Otherwise, the garden looked lifeless. Only the drip-drip of water.

Then Billy's eyes caught a small flurry of movement. Two sparrows on a branch, ruffling their feathers, trying to perk up in the dismal weather. One had a piece of grass in its beak. Had they started to nest?

That was what Mr Wainwright had meant that day. That life was everywhere, if you looked. That God was.

Really it was the same as Mrs Drury was always going on about – grass and leaves and stones, and sacred groves and all that. Even on a day like this life was trying to perk itself up. Things were happening, maybe underground, where you couldn't see. Leaves were already starting to grow, even if you couldn't see them.

Life was always fizzing up, Billy thought, *like the bubbles in a pop bottle*.

'You out there, Billy?' called his grandma. 'Put the kettle on. We'll have a nice cup of tea.'

Later that afternoon an idea came into his head.

'And was Uncle Ronnie fond of Foxcover?' he asked Grandma.

'Not specially, not that I can recollect,' said Grandma.

'Except at the end,' said Mr Wainwright.

'That's right, Tommy! Fancy you remembering that! People *did* say he was seen once down at Foxcover during his last leave – with a lass.'

'More than once,' said Mr Wainwright.

'Mebbies,' admitted Grandma.

98

'What doing?'

'Bit of slap and tickle,' laughed Mr Wainwright.

'Nothing of the sort!' said Grandma. 'Don't you start putting wrong ideas in the lad's head. Our Ronnie wasn't like that.'

'Who was the girl?' asked Billy.

'We never knew, Billy. If there was a girl.'

'There *was* a girl!' said Mr Wainwright. 'You know nicely! It was that lass from Crag End way, Tommy Barber's daughter.'

'That's what people said!'

'Very quiet lass, never had her head out of a book. She ended up in America.'

'Australia.'

'One of them places.'

'Funny thing is we lived in Charity Street at the time and if she met him that often how come I never once saw her walking along towards the Old Line? It was a mystery. Another bit of seed cake, Billy?'

Billy didn't ask any more questions after that.

He just sat and smiled as he forced the third piece of seed cake in. He wasn't smiling because the seed cake tasted good – though it did. And he wasn't smiling because he knew Grandma was fibbing again – which she was. Or because he'd guessed that Mr Wainwright had spoken something like the truth – which he had.

He was smiling because he felt that Uncle Ronnie had given him an answer now. Not in his own words, or course, but out of the mouths of Grandma and Mr Wainwright.

* * *

His dad came for him at six and they travelled down in Mr Brunsdon's car. Mr Brunsdon was over the moon because they'd managed to persuade all the maintenance staff to turn back at the factory gate.

'We'll whack 'em, Dick!' he kept saying. 'We'll whack 'em yet!'

He nearly whacked a bus as they went round a corner.

Billy sat quiet, still smiling.

Grandma had asked him to go to church with her tomorrow.

But he wasn't going there. He was going somewhere else tomorrow.

And nobody was going to stop him.

But nobody!

Chapter 14

In fact nobody even tried to stop him.

All the way along the Old Line he didn't see a living soul. Only the ghosts of miners ahead of him, tripping and barging their way along as they played their so-called *runny-races*!

And nearly to Foxcover, one of Rancher Fletcher's goats. It was tethered on the bankside and as he passed, it gazed blankly down at him in that unsurprised way that goats have, almost as if he had expected him at nine o'clock of a Sunday morning.

It bleated at him in a mournful, inquiring way.

Billy bleated back, not mournfully though.

Just the opposite.

Since the moment he woke he'd felt cheerful. Even before he got out of bed he felt – he *knew* – that whatever had been weighing him down for the last few days had been suddenly shifted off his back.

He strode up the grassy incline to Foxcover and when he reached the edge of the trees stood for a minute or two looking back down the Old Line.

Not because he was afraid that somebody might be watching him.

He *had* been afraid, this last day or two. He realised that now, he admitted it to himself. But he wasn't going to let fear rule him any more.

In any case there was nobody following him, Or

was there? He *may* have caught a glimpse of somebody dodging down behind the cover of a gorse bush quite close to the goat. Or he may not.

It didn't matter anyhow.

The bell of St Luke's church started pealing in the far distance. His grandma would be putting on her white gloves and wondering where she'd last put her prayer book.

Billy went into the wood.

He went first to the big ash tree where the Lookout Post was. He climbed up the six-inch nails that he and Elvis and Butcher had hammered into the trunk months back. There were other more rusted nails already there when they did the job, and Billy remembered flattening them into the bark.

Now he was standing in the Lookout Post, looking down. The boards under his feet were the ones he and Emma had put there after the last time the Crag Enders had wrecked the place. Even the bracken strewn on the floor was the same.

But it didn't feel the same to Billy. It felt different somehow.

Or perhaps it was that the Lookout Post was the same, and *he* was different? Was that it?

At any rate, he felt he didn't belong there any more. In a way, he had no right to be there any more. Not in the Lookout Post.

Foxcover, though, still belonged to him. He kept telling himself that as he climbed back down to earth. The Lookout Post belonged to the Gang. And he didn't belong in the Gang any more. But

Foxcover was different. Foxcover belonged to nobody. Or was it everybody?

At any rate it didn't belong to Cliffy Butcher.

He crossed the clearing (that Joey had made a touch too circular in his mural) and took the path that went past the big holly tree.

He kept his eyes skimmed for a fox as he walked. And he kept sniffing the air because Mr Wainwright had told him you could often smell where a fox was when you could never see one. He neither saw nor smelt one as he walked to the far end of the Wood. But that didn't mean there wasn't a fox there. These old names must mean something, Mr Wainwright had said, and folks weren't daft in them days. They wouldn't call it Foxcover for nowt. Just like the Old Line had once been a railway line carrying coal from Shilton Colliery to Belton railway station. In some ways, Mr Wainwright had said, the surest sign you have there's a fox about is when you can't see one.

It seemed a daft thing to say. But, perhaps the truth often was daft?

He was at the south side of the wood now, looking out across the field towards Morgan's farm. He had a good view of the old trackway that led past The Bone House (now a heap of rubble, but Billy's grandma could remember when bonemeal was made there) and then vanished over the brow of the hill to Lane Head House on the Bishop Auckland road.

There was no mystery, really, about how Uncle Ronnie's girlfriend had managed to meet him without being seen. If she'd scrambled up the side of Crag End sand quarry (not too difficult for a young lass) she had only to cross two fields and then she was on to the trackway, just beside the ventilation shaft from the old mine.

It was the way the Crag Enders had come when they wrecked the Lookout Post. Easy-peasy. That's why it was nuts to think you could guard it.

Two crows winged their way together over the field where spring wheat was already growing.

Maybe Uncle Ronnie had stood in this selfsame spot almost fifty years ago. Waiting for his girlfriend to come walking down the trackway. He probably waved to her as she passed The Bone House. She would be able to see him by then. He probably stood in this very spot. There was a good view, at the same time you couldn't be seen. That was likely what Uncle Ronnie had wanted.

Question: Why had he not wanted to be seen? Why had he not wanted his mother to know about the girl?

Answer: Maybe there were some questions you never got an answer for.

All that was a long time ago, of course. Did that mean it no longer mattered?

There was no girl on the track now. Nobody. But Billy could picture her.

In his imagination she was walking away from him. A slim girl, brown hair, a bit shy – like Michelle Wright. She turned and waved just before she passed The Bone House. Then she vanished beyond the trees of the hedgerow. Mebbies that was how Uncle Ronnie had last seen her.

After a moment he made his way back to the clearing and stood for a moment quietly thinking.

It was an old place, Foxcover. *Long, long ago, before the church was built and the yew trees planted* . . . That was how Grandma often started her stories. Foxcover was even older than that. It wasn't just Uncle Ronnie and before that Grandad and Grandma doing their courting and before that Mr Wainwright's father seeing a big white rat when he was young – he said it was a King Rat. The holly tree that Billy stood beside now was donkey's years old and before that holly tree there would be another one and before that . . .? Mrs Drury said there were trees in Foxcover five hundred years old. And before them there would be other trees? And before them?

It wasn't just the living things that inhabited Foxcover. There were the ghosts, the memories, all the things that had happened in the past, that could take you back through time.

Uproot the trees, rip out the bushes, and would the ghosts and memories be lost as well? Would something be snapped? Forever?

He wished that his grandma would sign Mrs Drury's petition.

He remembered the way Uncle Ronnie had spoken to him yesterday.

He wondered if trees could speak to you. If they were speaking to you all the time, really, only nobody ever listened to them.

He stood there, listening. And that was a strange thing: there wasn't a sound. You'd expect there to be some sound if you stood in the middle of a wood. But there wasn't. Not one bird called out. Not one leaf stirred. Not one blade of grass.

Then he realised what was happening. It wasn't that he was listening to the wood: the wood was listening to *him*. Waiting.

What was it waiting for?

As he looked, he saw something for the first time. Each tree, each bush, each branch, each leaf was different. Individual. Just like himself. Before, the bushes had seemed, well – just bushes. Now he saw they weren't. Each one was as unique as himself. They seemed to be presences. They seemed to have lives of their own.

And perhaps they did. Perhaps these bushes and trees, and even the stones under the ground, lived a life of their own. A life people only guessed at now and again. A life lived on a different timescale from our own. A long, slow, timescale that stretched back to beyond the beginning of time itself. And perhaps their lives were lived so slowly that human beings – whose lives were lived so fast – made the mistake of thinking that because they didn't notice them these things had no lives at all.

Perhaps they, too, suffered in some way, and smiled, like people. Maybe, in their own way, they also fell in love, cried, fought wars, and died in battle. Maybe they even had memories, memories that stretched further back than even Grandma's? Maybe . . .

It was a long time before the wood stopped speaking to him. Because that was how it seemed to him.

106

Perhaps, he thought, the voices he heard had come from his own head?

Perhaps that was another question that would never be answered.

A leaf stirred in the wind. A bird sang. Billy smiled.

When he left the shelter of the wood and stepped down onto he Old Line he saw Butcher walking along towards him swinging his stick.

And Billy felt glad.

Chapter 15

'Take yer coat off!' Butch said.

He was already scrambling up the bankside.

Billy followed him.

They were in a circle of flatness where the goat had been tethered the day before – it was almost as if it had been made for a fight.

The goat, a few yards down from them, looked up with its stony eyes and nodded three times at Billy.

You're right there, mate, thought Billy.

He folded his zipper-jacket and laid it tidily on the grass. Butch had already thrown his down.

'This is going to hurt you, Robinson!'

'Mebbies!' said Billy. 'Mebbies not!'

'No mebbies about it.'

Butch rolled up his sleeves and took up a pose.

'Ready?' he said.

Billy hadn't planned what he would do. He had known he was going to have to fight Butch since yesterday, suspected that it was Butch lurking in the gorse bushes when he had seen something blue a few minutes back, but he still hadn't planned things out.

'Attack's the best form of defence,' Mr Wainwright had said. Another of his nutty sayings. But this one sounded almost like common sense.

And it would get things over with. The worst part of going to the dentist's was always the waiting. Imagining the drill whining, touching a nerve, making you leap nine feet out of the padded chair. The dentist saying, 'Sorry about that, old chap, I forgot to give you an injection!' The actual being there, in the dentist's chair. was never that bad.

So Billy rushed straight in.

Not that it did him a lot of good.

He got a smart thump on the top of the head.

They circled about for a bit after that, Butch's long arms snaking out, making him keep his distance.

Got to get inside those long blinking arms! thought Billy. *Got to!*

But even when he managed it, stepping inside Butch's guard with a bit of nifty footwork, it didn't help him much. It was true he got a few solid blows into Butch's ribs. But it was like punching a sack of spuds. Worse!

That was the trouble with Butch. He didn't *have* any feelings, he didn't seem to feel pain, not like other people, normal people. It wasn't just that he could hand out punishment, he could take it as well. In a way it was what he was designed for. He was a big insensitive lump!

Punch! Punch! Punch! Billy hammered into his ribs.

Butch just laughed. He pushed Billy away with an almost contemptuous flick of his arms that made Billy rock back on his heels.

'A real fight, Robbo! No messing about!'

Billy circled him. He swung three or four punches that were either brushed aside or missed completely. But at least Butch hadn't landed a real blow on him yet.

Billy was just recovering his breath, just gaining in confidence, wondering where to aim his next blow – when Butch's fist flew out from nowhere and slammed straight into his mouth.

Billy felt the salt taste of blood, and a sudden arc of pain ran round the top of his mouth.

'Taste that, Robbo!' laughed Butcher.

Worse than the hurt of the blow, though, Billy felt the old fear leap to life again within him, a cold icicle of fear that knifed into his stomach and made him catch his breath.

Only for a moment, though. Billy remembered Mr Wainwright telling him how he'd laid big fellers out because of his will to win. He grabbed hold of that thought, clung on to it. And the thought of Foxcover, of Uncle Ronnie, of being forced back and back until you had nowhere to go.

And something else cheered him. The blow hadn't hurt that much. Not as much as he might have expected. It was *just* like going to the dentist's, really.

Neither did the next blow. Or the next. Or the next.

Billy's ears and jaw and mouth were burning now. A thump in the chest had all but winded him.

But it was always the same. They didn't hurt enough. Not enough to stop him.

And Billy realised something else now.

He was going to get one back at Butcher. He was going to make the big silly fool sit up and take notice.

Billy's eyes were wet with tears by now. But he didn't care. His mouth and nose were dripping blood, but that didn't seem to matter. There was something inside him now. Something hard and angry. Something that wanted to hurt Butcher. Something driving Billy on. And it wasn't going to stop.

He took another two punches on the arm, then when Butch swung wildly he stepped inside his arm and delivered a really good punch. A hook to the jaw. He felt it sink in, he knew he'd hurt Butch. It was exactly like the punch Leon Leroy had delivered to the American beerbelly. Well, maybe not exactly. But enough to make Butch shudder and utter a surprised *Ohhh!*

'You're blinking well for it now, Robinson!'

He dropped his guard and rushed straight at Billy. The ferocity of the attack quite overcame Billy. He staggered back and back, taking blows all the time. He couldn't see clearly. He caught glimpses of goat and sky and fist and grass in bewildering succession, then realised he was lying flat on his back with Butch on top of him, his legs straddling his chest, his long arms pinioning Billy's down in the grass above his head.

'Give in?' Butcher gasped, chest heaving.

Billy shook his head from side to side. He hadn't the breath to speak. There was blood and sweat and spit all over his face.

Butch climbed off him carefully, walked backwards a few paces, then stood ready.

112

Billy sucked in air. His head began to clear. He rubbed the tears from his eyes, then got to his feet.

He could hardly see anything as he rushed at Butch, both arms flailing. He felt two punches go into Butch's face, and another. He felt Butch stagger back, and Billy pushed on, elated, enjoying it, wanting to hurt Butch and—

Something hit him. Something hard, from outer space.

Billy seemed to float in the air for a long time. A long, long time above the grass and the goat and . . . and then he seemed to float off somewhere else . . . somewhere where there were stars in his head . . .

'Here's yer coat.' It was Butch speaking. He seemed a long way off. 'You all right?'

Billy opened his eyes. The blackness faded. Butch was standing over him. The sky behind his head was blue.

Billy opened his mouth to speak. He meant to say something sensible. But the words came out all wrong.

'Where did I go to?' he asked. What a stupid thing to say!

'Want a hand?' said Butch.

Billy felt a draught by his face. He realised Butch must have dropped his jacket beside him. He managed to sit up, though it made his head swim.

He saw Butch pick up his stick. Then start down the bankside.

He stopped and turned:

'Was a good fight, Robbo,' he said. He smiled and licked some blood from his cheek. 'You did good. Better than Benson! You're back in the Gang again, now, Robbo. So long!'

Chapter 16

That should have been the end of it.

But it wasn't.

Billy's answer to Butch's last words was to shake his head.

He nipped into the quarry to wash his face before he went home. He didn't want his mam yammering-on.

Not that it did any good.

His mam saw him through the kitchen window as he crossed the yard and he could hear her playing heck even before he'd set foot in the house.

'What on earth have you been doing, Our Billy!' she said as he came through the door. 'As if I hadn't enough on my plate already – without you starting on!'

'What's up?'

'What's up? Your dad's been involved in a scuffle on the picket line!' Billy could see his dad's coat on the chair-back, the sleeve torn off. 'And as if that wasn't bad enough Steven's pit has come out on strike. Then you walk in here like that!'

'Leave the lad alone, Alice,' said Billy's dad, who had come to the doorway of the other room. 'Can't you see he's been in a fight?'

'Fight! Fight! It's all you men think of!'

'Don't get het up, lass,'

'Have you been in a fight, Billy?'

'No, mam.'

'Well, I don't know! What have you been doing?'

'Fell off a tree.'

He wandered off into the other room before his mam could ask any more awkward questions.

'Who have you been fighting?' his dad asked. He'd sat down again in his chair by the fire. There was a snooker match on the telly.

Billy hesitated only a second.

'Cliffy Butcher.'

'Don't tell lies to your mother, Billy. All right? Or anybody else for that matter. Speak the truth and shame the devil, son, even if it is a bit awkward at times. Did you win?'

Billy shook his head. He couldn't admit it in words. Even the thought brought tears to the brink of his eyes again.

'You can't win them all, Billy. And Cliffy Butcher'll be a hard nut to crack. All the Butchers are. It's bred in the bone wi' them. They don't give up easy. That's how they win medals, son.'

'So you *have* been fighting?' said Billy's mother. She had come to the doorway.

'The lad's tekkin' enough beatin' for one day, Alice.'

'Shouldn't've got himself involved in a fight in the first place.'

'You can only run so far in this world,' said Billy's dad.

'Humph!' said his mother. 'What good did fighting do you last time?' She must have been talking about the strike before they shut the colliery down.

'It's not a question of good, Alice.'

116

'What is it a question of, then? That's what I'd like to know!'

Before his dad could answer she swung away and sailed back into the kitchen where a pan was threatening to bubble over.

'Well, I'm sorry you got whacked, son, but when all's said and done it's best to get these things off your chest and settled with.'

Billy concentrated on the snooker match. One chap was winning the frame by seventy-two points to six and was already three frames up. Billy felt like the other feller looked. Shaky. White-faced. All of a tremble.

'I fancied you had something on your mind last Saturday when we were up the allotment. You seemed – touchy. That's what for I told you that tale about Harry Duggan.'

Billy looked at his dad. He remembered the tale now. Harry Duggan, the fireman, having to climb the rigging when he went in the Navy as a lad. Halfway up he had looked down to the deck far below and fear had gripped him. For several seconds he was frozen to the rigging. His legs had shook. He felt sure he'd fall off. But he'd forced himself to climb over the top yardarm. And then, all those years later he won a medal for rescuing a man from the top of a block of flats.

Billy hadn't seen the point of the story when he first heard it.

'Thought you didn't twig on at the time,' his dad said. 'But I knew something had a hold on you.' He looked across at Billy. 'Some sort of fear.'

'I *wasn't* frightened, Dad!'

'Weren't you, son? Fair enough. Did I ever tell you I once fought Tommy Butcher?'

Billy looked across at his dad with sudden interest.

'It was a long time ago. And I don't mind admitting, I was frightened to death, Billy. Nearly thirty years ago it was.'

'And what happened?'

'It was over a lass. We both wanted to marry the same lass. I was going out with her at the time and Tommy Butcher didn't like it.'

'So what happened?'

'We fought each other for her. Behind The Red Lion. Years ago they used to have bare-knuckle fights there, and before that bear-baiting, so I heard tell. There was a bookie and fellers were making bets.'

'And who won?'

'Who do you think? Tommy Butcher massacred me, man. I never stood a chance. Fortunately, not a lot put their money on me. It was a bad day for the bookie! He had to find a proper job for a fortnight.'

'And what happened after that?'

'Tommy give us a hand-up off the floor and practically carried us across to see Dr Mitchell. I wasn't fit to travel far meself, like!'

'So he beat you?'

'Fair and square.'

'And he married the girl?'

'No, Billy. *I* married the girl.'

'But I thought you said –'

'So I did, Billy. Girls don't always go for winners

118

you know. Women might look all frills and lipstick but there's some of them got a bonny lot of sense!'

'It's just a pity you can't listen to a bit of it, then!' Billy's mam shouted from the kitchen. 'If you two's finished jawing mebbies one of you could bother to lay that table in there!'

'Mind, sometimes, Billy,' said his dad getting up to get the tablecloth out of the drawer, 'I sometimes wish I'd won the fight. I bet Tommy Butcher doesn't have to set the table on a Sunday!'

And he winked at Billy.

Chapter 17

What his dad said made Billy feel better about Butch. Not a lot. But slightly.

And it tickled him to think that Butch had offered to yank him to his feet, just like his dad had done all those years ago with Billy's dad.

It was as if they were out of the same mould, as if Butch was just a carbon copy of his dad. It was what Mrs Drury called history repeating itself. That was why she'd been so pleased that Joey had put Foxcover and the Old Line and even the quarry den into his mural of the ancient Greeks.

Except, of course, it wasn't an exact copy of the fight between the Butchers and the Robinsons. This time they weren't fighting over a girl – were they?

When the thought first occurred to him there was only one girl sprang to his mind. Emma Ward. Before all this business he quite liked her. As far as Billy knew Butch had never so much as given her a second glance.

Not that Billy cared. Nowadays he didn't give twopence for Emma Ward.

She was waiting for him at the school gate on Monday morning. She gave him a big smile. Even spoke to him. Cheek! 'How do, Billy!' As if nothing had happened, as if she wasn't to blame for it all!

He ignored her, of course.

Mr Starr saw him in the corridor going to registration.

'What happened to your eye, Billy?' he asked.

'Bumped into a door, sir,' said Billy.

'Oh, yes? And what was the door called?'

Mr Starr had already walked on.

But just before morning break he called Billy into his office again.

'This door you bumped into,' he said, 'it wasn't by any chance Clifford Butcher?'

'Yes, sir.'

'I hope there isn't anything between you two idiots?'

'No, sir.'

'It's all over, is it? You know he's in the team? And I don't want to lose this match tomorrow. You understand. Billy? I don't want to humiliate them like we did last time – I don't want that at all – but losing's a different matter. You take my meaning?'

'Sir.'

'And you've been getting some practice in like I asked you to?'

'Sir.'

'I expect Clifford won the fight, did he?'

Billy nodded.

'How many rounds did you last?'

'About three minutes.'

'You must be tougher than you look! Now forget all about it.'

Out in the yard Billy joined in the kickabout for the first time in a week. He played with Daz and they won easy-peasy. Billy was in brilliant form.

There were some days when he was unstoppable. As he put over another fantastic cross he thought they'd win by four or five goals tomorrow.

Butch wasn't playing at first, but when he did roll up he didn't bother throwing his weight about this time. Just played a normal game: well, normal for him. Even though stupid Slattery kept whispering something in his ear. Probably egging him on to trip Billy or Daz up. But Butch took no notice.

In fact, Billy was almost beginning to think it really was all over between them. That Butch was okay after all. Almost human.

That was the night more trouble occurred on the picket line.

Billy was down there with his dad, he saw it all, but it was still impossible to be sure what happened.

For a start off, it was dark. And the headlights of the lorry were shinning straight into their eyes.

The lorry driver had got down from his cab to talk to Mr Butcher and two other pickets. They were standing a few yards from the lorry, by the factory gates. Mr Butcher was getting narked. A few choice swear words flew through the air. But the lorry driver, a dark stocky man, wasn't taking a lot of notice. Three policemen were standing on the edge of the pavement across the main road, like runners waiting for the off.

Billy, his dad, and six or seven other pickets were warming themselves round the brazier.

Mr Brunsdon – who had been reading them the

123

evening paper ('Not a mention of the strike, lads! Not a dicky bird! That's the capitalist press for you! We might as well not exist as far as these fellers are concerned!') was standing between the brazier and the gates talking to Mr Hyslop who had arrived minutes earlier.

Mr Hyslop was wearing a posh new padded coat and even a hat! Billy had never seen him looking so smart. He seemed confident and smiling. He even shook everybody's hand – he even shook Billy's! – and told them it wouldn't be long now before they won.

'One more week, lads,' he said. 'The main thing is to stick together.'

Now he and Mr Brunsdon were watching the argument by the gate.

'Look, mate,' Mr Butcher was saying, 'why don't you just climb into that lorry of yours and get back down south where you belong, eh? You have no idea what conditions is like up here, man! I'm asking you for the last time!'

He looked just like Butch did when he got wild. Eyes bulging, face red, like a bomb about to go off.

Mr Brunsdon came over towards the brazier. For some reason he chucked his newspaper in it. It seemed a daft thing to do to Billy. Somebody might have like to read it. The paper was immediately engulfed in a roar of flames. 'Keep that fire blazing, lads,' he said, then he went back to Mr Hyslop.

The pair of them walked towards the gate. By now Tommy Butcher had taken his hands out of his pockets. They looked like they might do something dangerous any minute. Mr Hyslop took Mr Butcher by the arm and moved him quietly away round the front of the lorry.

Very sensible, Billy thought. Otherwise there might have been trouble.

Meanwhile Mr Brunsdon was talking to the driver. Talking very quietly and reasonably, for Mr Brunsdon. He only wagged his prize sausage finger twice.

'We're askin' you in the name of reason, man, as a fellow human bein''—

That was when it happened.

There was an almighty crash.

It was a second or so before Billy realised that the windscreen of the cab had been smashed.

The police whistle went and three bobbies charged across the road. As they did so the lorry driver fell to the ground and at the same time Mr Brunsdon went round the front of the lorry. A tick later he was coming back with Mr Hyslop and at the same time Mr Butcher went under the lorry and came out at the side where the bobbies grabbed him.

One policeman's helmet went flying, a second said a word Billy never thought policemen said, and then between the three of them they had Mr Butcher under control, more or less. Mr Brunsdon was shouting to the pickets who had rushed from the brazier. 'Steady, lads, no violence, please! Cool it! Hoo! Stop it, you lot!' He was walking back towards the brazier as Billy passed him on his way to his dad who was already tending to the lorry driver.

'I seemed to fall over my own feet,' the lorry driver was saying, 'then something hit me on the head.'

'Fancy that!' said Billy's dad helping him to his feet.

The scuffling was dying down. The police were looking for whatever had been used to bung the windscreen through. They were searching Mr Hyslop, his coat was open. 'You'll find nothing on me, constable,' he was saying. One bobby was under the lorry. Another was searching Mr Butcher for the third time.

Billy and his dad wandered back to the brazier.

'I'll be off, then, Matty,' said Billy's dad.

'Off? This is no time to be deserting a sinking ship!' said Mr Brunsdon, turning round. He had been warming his hands, standing with his broad back to all the commotion.

Billy saw why now: in the flames of the brazier there was something still visible, a stout piece of wood, that could have been a pick-shaft, fast burning away.

'I told you before we started, Matty, no violence, or else —'

'What violence? There's been no violence that I know of!'

'That driver could've been badly hurt, Matty. He thinks he fell over his own feet, but we all know better than that, don't we?'

'I don't know what you're on about!'

'Don't you? I expect an old professional wrestler can mek anybody fall over his own feet when he wants them to!'

126

Mr Brunsdon grinned.

Billy knew what had happened now. After tripping the driver, Mr Brunsdon had gone round the other side of the lorry, collected the pick-shaft from Tommy Butcher and quietly made his way back to the brazier. Clever!

'You're not leaving, Dick?' asked Mr Hyslop as he came over.

' 'Fraid so, Archie,' said Billy's dad. 'I told Matty here before we started I wanted no violence, so that's that!'

'I do so deplore violence,' said Mr Hyslop.

'Do you?' asked Billy's dad, looking him square in the eye. 'Do you really, Archie?'

Chapter 18

Right from the start the match went wrong.

Even before the match.

When Billy went to the bogs before he got on the minibus he saw the writing on the door was finished now: ROBINSON LUVS WARDY TRUE it said.

And then as he climbed on to the minibus Wardy was sitting near the front and she smiled at him again and said, 'Think we going to win, Billy?'

'How the heck do I know!' he said, blushing.

'Ooooooh!' they all shouted at him and Slattery shouted from the back in his scoffy voice:

'Why don't you sit beside her, William?'

'That'll do, you hooligans!' shouted Miss Benfold, who was driving. 'Everybody here?'

'All except Butcher, miss and he's not all there!' said Elvis, and Butcher, who was sitting next to him, belted him one in the arm.

Billy sat next to Daz.

'Look at me boots,' Daz said. They had brand-new laces and he'd put butter on the soles and studs to stop his boots sticking in the mud. 'Me dad told us about that,' Daz said.

It seemed a waste of time to Billy. But they were a daft lot in Daz's house. They were the sort of people who never failed to buy a dog licence, and

128

129

Daz's dad wasn't permitted in the house without his slippers on.

Still, Billy had to admit it was one stage better than Butcher who all the time Miss Benfold wasn't watching was stuffing himself with toffees. Probably give himself indigestion during the match. Probably nicked the toffees off some poor nut anyhow.

'Do you think we'll win, William?' Slattery kept shouting in his prissy voice (it was supposed to be like Emma Ward's but was nothing like) all the way to Middleham, and all his silly cronies from Mr Fixby's class kept laughing like a load of old crows.

As if that wasn't bad enough the match started off with a near disaster. The big striker hacked Billy down in the first minute and nearly went on to score. He only missed because he tripped over his own feet (which were like dustbins).

It was a really blatant foul. Really obvious. But the referee, a Middleham teacher, decided to ignore it. He kept looking at everybody sideways – like a duck – and had a college scarf that insisted on wrapping itself round his knees.

A second later when Daz was nearly kicked into Scotland by the Middleham fullback and Billy protested, the referee said, 'Play on or I'll book you!' and moved off with his sideways duck movement. 'Nobody's perfect!' he said, and Billy thought *You can say that again!*

Then there was Slattery, just behind Billy at left-back. He kept playing too wide out, leaving the middle of the field wide open, like a barn door. Billy told him twice in the first ten minutes, but Slattery told him to get stuffed and just laughed at him.

Then when Daz passed back to him, Billy – who had two men on him – let the ball go through to Slattery who was unmarked, and Slattery missed it and it went over for a corner.

'That was your ball!' Slattery said as they took their positions in the area.

'I left it for you!'

'You do your own dirty work, Robinson!'

Billy cleared the corner easily. He headed the ball out to Elvis who he'd noticed drop infield from the wing, and Elvis took it away safely.

It still worried Billy, though. It made him shaky to think that from now on he couldn't let a ball go through. It was possible that Slattery might even miss it on purpose. He was that sort of nut.

But there was something even worse.

As the game progressed he began to see one thing very clearly.

He was in the wrong position.

He could feel it in his bones. With every pass he made. Every time he blocked a pass.

It wasn't that he couldn't handle the big striker. He could do that blindfold.

And like he'd said to Mr Starr, he could tackle and intercept and push people off the ball. In the first five minutes he blocked a shot with his chest and cleared it upfield and in four tackles out of five he came away with the ball.

It wasn't that. Not that he hadn't the skill, the technique.

It was that he didn't feel right.

He didn't want to be blocking, stopping, frustrating ideas all the time, ending movements.

He wanted to be *creating* movements, making openings, putting balls through, seeing where chances were for doing things.

He hadn't noticed that before about himself. You didn't notice in kickabout games, where things didn't matter.

But in crucial situations you did notice.

Not that he could do anything about it now.

He just had to make the best of it.

He chested down a pass to the big striker, shoved the ball past him, drew a man, then stroked it to Daz and resumed his place.

In a way it was Mr Starr's fault, Mr Starr who must have just arrived because he was now on the touchline.

Daz beat two men brilliantly, but then ran the ball into touch, dead unlucky.

'Come on, Billy!' shouted Mr Starr. He sounded none too pleased. Hadn't he noticed Billy's superb pass?

Billy put his heart into the game now. He put two good passes through to Butcher, but the big clot missed them. He didn't even bother to try for the second.

Then Billy robbed the big striker – it was like taking a dummy from a bairn – and after moving towards Emma Ward on the left swung the ball out to Elvis on the right instead.

132

Unfortunately, Elvis didn't notice. He was having an argument with the fullback, another big hacker.

What the heck was going on over there?

The game was getting scrappy, hardly two balls strung together most of the time. There was no rhythm in the game. It was just kick and run, not really football at all.

Billy took the ball off the big striker again (he was the only player of theirs who ever took passes: he'd obviously told the others he would belt them if they touched the ball. Probably a cousin of Butcher's!) and moved upfield to try and get things moving.

He pushed deep into their half, Emma Ward running ahead of him, calling for the ball. It was good, that, it drew a man.

Billy waited till Daz was clear, then put a ground ball through to him.

Daz was brilliant. He was right on the edge of the penalty area when he got the ball. He jiggled past one man, then a second, made the centre half look an idiot and then, just when he had a chance to score, for some reason turned round and beat all three men again! Billy had never seen anything like it. It was so brilliant. It was a tragedy really, when Daz collapsed with exhaustion, just outside the penalty box, a yard back from the position he'd first started from.

After that the game fell apart again. When the referee started looking at his watch a thought struck Billy. Last time they'd played Middleham they'd been winning 5-1 at half-time (Billy had scored the third goal). Even though Mr Starr had taken off Danny Howells – their star player – in the second half, they'd still run out 7–1 winners in the end. And here they were with nearly half the game gone and still only a goalless draw.

Maybe there was still time to do something about it.

Billy intercepted a pass to the big striker (he was the sort of kid who liked the ball delivered personally to his right toe-end) and started pushing upfield.

He beat a man and drew another. Daz called for the ball and Billy passed to him. Daz passed straight back to him, drawing him on. Billy went left. Again Emma Ward drew the back away and Billy and Daz did a brilliant one-two movement.

It was then that Billy made the decision.

He saw the ref put the whistle to his lips. It must be nearly time. Billy was tiring himself, and Butch was standing off screaming for the ball right in front of the goal. But Billy didn't want to waste another chance. *If you want a job doing properly*, his dad often said, *might as well do it yourself!*

Billy couldn't get a good view of the goal himself. He turned midfield. He went past one man, he drew back his right foot – and then a terrible thing happened.

Some player he hadn't noticed zoomed in and booted the ball away.

134

It was a hopeless hoof of a kick, no direction at all. But it happened – just happened – to go right to the big striker who was standing (still rooted to the spot, of course, waiting for a personal delivery) just beyond the halfway line, and he turned with the ball and headed for goal.

Billy couldn't believe what happened next.

Slattery was too far out to do anything. The other back seemed to do his best to get out of the way. The big striker rammed in a shot that spun off the side of his right dustbin – and the ball was in the net.

'Goal!' screamed the referee and he only just remembered to blow his whistle for half-time before he waddled upfield to clutch the big striker up in his wings and whirl him round with delight.

'Look, lad, what do you think you're doing?' asked Mr Starr.

He'd drawn Billy away from the others while Miss Benfold talked to them.

'Not my fault, sir.'

'Whose fault is it, then? It's your job to mark the central striker, isn't it?'

'That referee's not fair, sir.'

'He's not perfect,' said Mr Starr, 'that I will admit—'

'He should've blew up for time, sir.'

'Have you got a watch on you, Billy? Well, then, how do you know it was time? Leave that to him. Meanwhile you concentrate more on your own job

135

– all right? Now, look, we haven't got all day. Now listen, I want this match winning. First, you look after the defence. I want no more goals through. Second, what are you doing with Butcher?

'What you mean, sir?'

'Every pass you make to him is a bad one.'

'It's his fault, sir.'

'It's not, it's yours! Every pass you make him is either too short or too far ahead. You're trying to make the lad look a fool! Second, what's happening to Emma Ward? It was you that wanted her in the team in the first place and how many passes has she had since I've been here?'

'Don't know, sir.'

'You don't know because your mind's not on the job, lad. I could see that when I first arrived. You were in a dream. She's had two passes all the time I've been here, and do you know how many you've given her?'

'No, sir.'

'Not hard to count. Nil. None. Nix. Snap out of it, Billy! You hear me? You've got to play as a team. If you're going to starve anybody stop wasting passes to Darrell Thompson. He's that clever he ends up beating himself. Now, pull yourself together, lad. And one other thing. Get Bobby Slattery to drop infield. He's too far out.'

'I've told him, sir.'

'Well, tell him again! You're captain! And watch your mate.'

'Who'd you mean, sir?'

'Good God, Billy! Elvis Potter is your mate, isn't he?'

'He used to be, sir.'

'Whatever is the matter with you, lad? Haven't you noticed what's going on between him and that back? He'll get sent off if he's not careful, and we've had enough tragedies for one week! Now get back to Miss Benfold and listen to what she says!'

Elvis got sent off five minutes into the second half for kicking the big right-back. In a way it was fair. In another way it wasn't fair. It was six and two-threes with the pair of them, really. Or five and two-eights as Elvis put it. Nuts!

Billy felt sick when Elvis got his marching orders. For five minutes he was so mad he couldn't concentrate on the game at all.

What a pig's ear he was making of things! He remembered how good Bellwood was as a captain. How cool.

Then he pulled himself together. The game wasn't over yet. There was plenty of time for them to win. *The game isn't over till it's over*, Steven used to say. He remembered Harry Duggan up the rigging, struggling with his fear. *Come on! Come on!* he kept saying as he forced himself higher.

It was what Billy said to himself now.

First he shut down the centre completely. The big striker's cocky head started drooping. Then he told Slattery once and for all to stay in. This time, for some reason, Slattery took some notice.

Then, staying central, so no more slip-ups could occur, Billy started to dominate the match. He'd sent Daz out onto the right wing, where he took two defenders with him (by now they thought he was a Danger Man, the fools!)

Billy started feeding balls out to Emma. She did well. Gradually more and more pressure was put on the Middleham defence. They began to make mistakes. Defenders were being pulled out on to both wings to watch Emma and Daz, leaving Butch in the middle all alone.

At last Billy pushed a ground ball to Butch. He trapped it and turned. The defender was rushing in at him. Butch feinted to go left and—

Billy was amazed. Butch *went* to his left. Billy could hardly believe it. He actually *went to his left*. Probably for the first time in his entire career! The defender was wrong-footed. Butch was through to the six-yard box. The goalie – who must have been quite a sensible person – dived the wrong way, and the ball was in the net.

It was a lucky goal Butch had scored, of course, a mis-kick, really. But a goal. The two sides were back on equal terms now.

Five minutes later Billy's team scored the winning goal.

Slattery burst through on the left, going right down the wing. Emma cut inside and then took a pass from him. She turned, pushed the ball slightly to her left, and then put a really cool shot into the bottom of the goal. Before Billy realised what had happened Slattery had grabbed her and swung her round in his big clumsy arms.

Billy should have felt happy. But he didn't. He felt anger as he watched them. Emma getting swung round and clearly liking it. Red anger clouded his brain.

He wasn't quite sure why it was anger he felt at that moment. But that's what he *did* feel.

Chapter 19

The Arab's men had their backs to the sea now. As he spoke to the BBC correspondent he was surrounded by guards with sub-machine guns. 'We shall never leave this land,' he said. 'Here we fight, or die.' All the time he spoke his guards were anxiously scanning the buildings around them, their eyes wild and restless. Every building the camera showed was pock-marked by shells and bullets.

'I think you've had your chips, now, lad,' said Billy's dad, speaking to the Arab.

'Are you sorry, Dad?'

'I am and I'm not, son. I can see his point of view, like. Every feller wants a place to call his own. On the other hand . . .'

'I cannot mek head nor tail or it, meself,' said Billy's mam coming in from the kitchen where she was cooking his dad's favourite meal (fried kidney, bacon, and mushrooms). Now that he'd pulled out of the strike the pair of them were back on speaking terms. 'It's like this business in Northern Ireland.'

'That'll be going on there till Kingdom Come,' said Billy's dad.

At least the weather forecast was better. Sort of.

'This rather depressing depression which has been sitting on us all like a very wet blanket during the last few days has decided to push off somewhere else, so I think I can promise you all a spot of somewhat sunnier weather!'

'Thank the Lord for that!' said Billy's mam.

'However, before you all rush outside, let me just warn you that as well as being sunnier the next few days are going to be chillier.'

'I thought there'd be a snag!' said Billy's mam.

The lead story on the local news was about a feller in Seaham who had been unemployed for three years, and to pass the time usefully he had made a miniature mouth organ, stuck it through the bars of his budgie's cage (she was called Vera, after somebody called Vera Lynn), and had finally managed to train his budgie to blow on it.

It played a proper tune, which was either *Bluebells of Scotland* or *Edelweiss*, one of the two.

'How perfectly marvellous!' said Lord La-de-dah (whose mind little things tended to please). 'And how on earth did you manage that?'

'Why, I had a lot of time on me hands,' said unemployed feller from Seaham.

'Three years of it,' Billy's dad reminded him.

'And I couldn't 'a done it, like, without a lot of love and patience. Vera's had the free run of the house.'

That bit was true. You could tell by the state of the furniture. Especially the sofa back.

'Now isn't that a marvellous incentive for all you unemployed people out there?' asked Lord La-de-dah. 'Instead of just bemoaning your lot why not get off your backsides and give it a try?'

He flashed them a sparkling glimpse of his gnashers. They really were too perfect. Perhaps Grandma was right after all and they were false.

'Ah, lad, that'll solve all our problem up here,' said Billy's dad. 'Massed bands of a thousand unemployed budgies playin' *Land of Hope and Glory* for the last night of the proms!'

Then Valerie Figg started talking about the strike at the factory:

'Support for the strike seems to be ebbing away,' she was saying, looking down her nose at them, and forgetting they all knew her Uncle Wally, 'and now a man is being held at Durham police station to assist the police in their enquiries into the incident of violence that occurred last night.'

'That'll be Tommy Butcher!' chortled Billy's dad. 'They'll get a fat lot of assistance out of him!'

'How'd you mean, Dad?'

'Folks used to say that if only the Jerries had ever got their hands on Tommy Butcher's uncle the war would've been finished in five minutes.'

'How's that, Dad?'

'He was a paratrooper, wasn't he, Dick?'

'First in and last out at Arnhem. Corporal Stan Butcher. He got the Military Medal. They don't give them away for nowt!'

'But how would he have ended the war in five minutes?' asked Billy.

'Five minutes of Stan Butcher, son, and the

whole of the German army'd 'ave been begging for mercy. Hitler'd 'ave been on the hot-line to Churchill offering unconditional surrender. Same wi' Tommy. First help the Durham constabulary'll get from Tommy Butcher is when they send him back home so they can have a rest!'

'How long will he get in prison, Dad?'

'Eh? No time at all it's to be hoped!'

'But he did it.'

'Did what?'

'Knocked that feller's windscreen through.'

'He never did, Billy.'

'But I saw the pick-shaft in the fire, Dad. He must've give it to Mr Brunsdon.'

'Somebody did, Billy. It wasn't Tommy Butcher, though.'

'Who was it, then?'

'Archie Hyslop did it. What for you think he was wearing that padded jacket last night? Didn't you see him go round the front of the lorry, out of sight? That's when he did it. Tommy was only used as a diversionary tactic.'

'But will he own up it was him?'

'Not him, Billy. Talk sense. Archie Hyslop's on his way to the European Parliament now the union's finished. He knows what side his bread's buttered on. Tommy Butcher'll take the rap, if rap there is to be took. All the Butchers are like that. More brawn than brain. That's what for their oldest lad's out there in Northern Ireland now. He's had two bullets through him already in the Falklands. He'll get another afore he's

143

finished out there, mark my words. The government'll pin another medal on his chest and say Ta very much and he'll end up like his Uncle Stan.'

'How did he end up, Dad?'

'Two wooden legs, Billy, blown off at Arnhem, poor feller!'

All this made Billy think, of course. Not just about Butch's uncle and his dad and his brother. But about Butch as well.

Maybe if you had an uncle and a dad and a brother like that you couldn't help being a bit of a fist-merchant. Every time Billy thought of Butch it was of him doling out a bit of punishment.

But, really, he wasn't that bad – was he?

What had happened to make him change his mind? Billy wondered. Not just what he'd learnt about his uncle and that. Maybe it was what Mr Starr had said at half-time as well, about deliberately trying to make Butch look a fool.

Had he really tried to do that? Was it possible?

And when he thought about Butch's goal, it hadn't been too bad, not really.

When he'd first thought about it, it seemed a stupid goal. A fluke. But maybe it wasn't that bad. Maybe Butch had meant the ball to swerve in like that. He remembered practising his own banana and bendy shots up at the top of Wolsely on Friday night.

And when Butch had scored at least he hadn't

gone lolloping around plonking kisses on every-body – like some people. It was true he'd rushed up to Elvis on the touchline and swung him round three times like something on a merry-go-round before flinging him in the rough direc-tion of the referee. But, then, everybody wanted to throw Elvis in the rough direction of some-thing, and perhaps particularly, in the rough direction of a cheating referee. It was only natural.

Billy went around to see Elvis after the news.

Mrs Potter was wearing a new fur coat – Mr Potter had won a packet on a horse called Loopy-da-loup. She was still sitting on her wooden box, but she said she was getting used to it now.

'Like me coat, Billy?' she said. 'It's genuine imitation lambswool.'

She stood up and twirled around, nearly trampling the greyhound underfoot: it was a good job it was quick on the uptake, even if it was sluggish in movement.

'Lovely, Mrs Potter.'

She looked like an old retriever making its last stand on its back legs.

'Where's your Soss?' Billy asked Elvis when they went in the kitchen to play darts. The board was stuck on the back door and there were fifty million holes in it as if fifty million woodworms had been hard at work. If his mother's back door had been like that she'd have had a screaming fit.

'Emigrated,' said Elvis.

'Where?'

'She's always down the bakery now with them communists,'

'She wants to stop down there!' Mr Potter shouted through.

'I blame me dad's mouth,' said Elvis. 'It's bigger than Tynemouth!'

'What's that?' shouted Mr Potter.

'I'm just saying they come from down south,' said Elvis. 'Them folks from the bakery.'

Billy laughed that much he missed the board.

'Heard about our dog?' Elvis asked him. 'The other night it sat up and begged for ten pence.'

'What for?'

'To phone up the RSPCA,'

'Are you tellin' lies in there again?' his mam shouted through.

'No, Mam. Honest.'

'He's tellin' lies in there, isn't he, Billy?'

'When does he ever tell owt else?' asked Mr Potter.

'What for'd it want to phone the RSPCA?' Billy asked him.

'Bribe them to tek it back again!'

'What lies you telling now, Our Elvis?'

'I'm just saying me dad's got his back again! What's up wi' yer lugs out there?'

'By God, my back's givin' me some josh!' Mr Potter said.

'There'll be summat the matter wi' *your* lugs when I come out there, young man!' said Mrs Potter.

147

'Never gerroff yer bum!'

'EH? WHAT DID YOU SAY?'

'I've just scored hundred and one!'

'I don't know what! Come in here a minute, Billy, and talk to us.'

Billy went to the doorway.

Mrs Potter was reading a book called *She Did It All For Love*. There was a picture on the front of a slim woman in white driving a carriage up to the front of a posh house.

'Like me book, Billy?' She held up the book for him to see. 'I think this is one of the best books ever written, I really do. It's all true, about the lass that starts off as a skivvy and ends up married to a duke. Men keep trying to take advantage of her – know what I mean, Billy? – because she's that good looking. I'd like to model meself on her if I could.'

'What for don't you get yersel down to *His and Hairs* next Monday,' said Mr Potter.

'Mebbies I will.'

'Mek yersel look decent.'

'We 'aven't always had plenty of lolly, Billy, but we've got it now!' said Mrs Potter.

'They tell me they're closing your Steven's pit down Barnsley way,' said Mr Potter. 'Is that right?'

'Don't know, Mr Potter.'

'Your turn,' said Elvis, coming in and handing him the darts.

Billy went back into the kitchen. He hadn't heard anything definite about Steven's pit closing down. And neither had his mother. He knew

148

that because she was still smiling when he left the house. That didn't mean it wasn't true. The Potters seemed to have advance warning of these matters. It was a certain fact that Mrs Potter had known Billy's sister was going to have a baby before Billy's sister had known it herself. It was no wonder they never bothered to watch the news.

'Great goal Butch scored,' said Elvis, coming back in.

'Bit fluky.'

'He's been practising them benders all week, man.'

'You sure?'

'Positive. You comin' back in the Gang now?'

'I might.'

'You want to. We gonna get the Crag Enders tomorrow night.'

'How d'you mean?'

'We gonna nobble them. Butch has this plan. They comin' up to Foxcover to wreck the Lookout Post. We gonna trap them.'

Same old plan!

'Slattery told us.'

'What's he know about it?'

'Reckons he knows.'

'He would.'

'You comin'?'

'Depends.'

'What's up? Still not pals with Butch?'

'He shouldn't have done that to Benson.'

'What you on about?'

'Mek him eat dirt.'

'He never.'

'He did!'

'He didn't, man. He *pretended* he was gonna mek Benson eat it, and then he made Cloughy eat it instead.'

'Are you sure?'

'Positive. So you coming back in the Gang? We got this great rope-ladder now, to keep the enemy out. Eh, Billy?'

Chapter 20

Billy was still pondering that question when they were having a kickabout before going into school next morning.

This time he played with Elvis instead of Daz, and they won easy. He could see Mr Starr had been right about Daz. He was all flash and no performance.

Butch joined in at the end. Billy had to tackle him twice and once Butch blocked one of his shots. But there didn't seem to be any hard feelings, at least not on Butch's part. He even clapped Billy on the back.

Billy still didn't feel exactly right. Not *exactly*. He didn't know why. He just didn't.

It was Emma he felt sorry for, though.

She hovered on the edge of the game the whole time, obviously wanting to join in. Out of the corner of his eye Billy had noticed in the last few days how she'd been gradually detaching herself from Deborah Padget and the rest of The Lipstick Brigade.

Which showed a *bit* of sense.

He only wished he could have asked her to join in. But he couldn't. Not after what was written on the bog door. And all that shouting on the minibus.

The mural was finished now. Everybody in the class had something on the wall, even

Millicent Pringle who could hardly draw her breath and Elvis who had two pin-goats on the skyline, but the bulk of it – and the great look it had – was all due to Michelle and Joey.

'I think the pair of them deserve a little clap, don't you?' said Mrs Drury, pausing at Billy's table as she gathered in their final Cadmus stories.

Everybody clapped. Michelle Wright blushed red. Joey tried to look modest and kept his eyes fixed down on the table-top, only the edges of his mouth showing how totally chuffed he really was.

He had good right to be. The last scene was great. Full of threat. Three of the five surviving warriors had their backs to you, so you couldn't really see their faces.

All you could see was their broad shoulders, their leather armour, their heavy dangerous hands holding their swords ready to strike or sheathe. You could see Cadmus was taking a real big chance. In another second they might easily overwhelm him.

It was the fact that you couldn't see their faces that made them look so dangerous and unpredictable. Faceless, like warriors often

were. Maybe Joey had got the idea of the picture off a Greek helmet Mrs Drury had stuck on the wall last week. At first you thought it had eyes. But they weren't eyes. They were just holes; holes that saw nothing.

The face of Cadmus was looking out at you, and at the five remaining warriors. There was no doubt about whose face it was now. Anybody in the school would have recognised that face.

Even Mrs Drury recognised it.

'And Cadmus has the look of somebody we all know well,' she said, glancing at Butch.

'Miss, is it Princess Di?' asked Alison Fretwell.

'Not quite, dear. Would you like to be a soldier, Clifford, like your brother?'

'Wouldn't mind, miss.'

'How is he getting on in Northern Ireland?'

'Sez it's a doddle, miss. Sez there's nowt goin' on.'

Everybody laughed. Billy looked across at Butch and almost managed to smile at him.

'Well, I'm glad to hear it. No doubt your mother'll be pleased.' She turned back to the mural. 'I particularly like the suggestion of the city Cadmus is going to build tucked away in these clouds here, almost like a dream.' It would have been easy to miss. Joey rolled his eyes when Billy looked across at him. He always did that when he was embarrassed. 'Well, I think it's very good, Michelle and Joey. Very good indeed.'

It was.

Billy only hoped she'd think the same about his story. He'd put his heart and soul into the writing on Sunday night, especially the fighting bit.

Not that he had much hope. Soskiss always won.

'It's a funny thing how on this table some people seemed determined to be silly,' Mrs Drury said as she gathered up the papers from Billy's table.

She was probably referring to Elvis's drawing which showed the Delphic Oracle with a word bubble coming out of its mouth saying *Follow the bear!* But by the way she looked she obviously included the rest of them – Billy, Joey and Daz – in the criticism as well.

Just because you sat next to somebody it didn't mean you were supposed to be the same as them, did it? It wasn't fair.

Mr Starr sent for him just before the bell went for break. Billy didn't relish going to see the headmaster again. He didn't fancy another telling-off.

'We nearly lost the match yesterday, Billy,' said Mr Starr. 'Do you know whose fault that was?'

'Mine, sir.'

'No. Mine, Billy. I thought it was yours yesterday, but I was wrong. I should have overruled you when you wanted to put Darrell in the team. I should have known better. But we all do something daft in our lifetimes. Perhaps we're fated to.'

He laughed and looked across at Billy.

'Which reminds me, Miss Benfold was in only a minute ago and we were talking about the first time we made Bellwood captain. He was about your age, in Mrs Drury's. Know how he played?'

'Good, sir?'

'Hopeless. He completely went to pieces. We lost 2-1. That surprise you?'

'Sir.'

'And the second time we drew against a poor team. But we persevered with him. He's captain of the area schools' team next week. Did you know that?'

'No, sir.

Mr Starr smiled down at him.

'He's a natural captain, Billy, like you. But everybody has to learn. This business with you and Clifford Butcher patched up now?'

'Nearly, sir.'

'Just let me say this, Billy. I'd written you off yesterday, at half-time. We were losing, and we deserved to be. But you turned that game round, Billy Robinson. You pulled the fat out of the fire, and I was wrong. I don't mind admitting that. I was just being daft again. As far as I'm concerned you're still in there with a chance. Maybe everybody deserves a second chance. Everybody. You understand my meaning?'

'Sir.'

'One other thing, Billy. If we do have you as captain next year you'll be playing as striker, no doubt about that. You're a maker, Billy, not a breaker. I saw that yesterday. In my day the captain was always in defence. But those days are gone now. I should have known. Everything changes, Billy. Even football. We're all part of the big wheel. Understand? You will do one day. Off you go now, lad. And well done!'

All day Billy thought about Mr Starr's words.

He wasn't too sure what *the big wheel* bit meant. But at least the smarting inside him started to heal.

It was still daft, what the Gang was doing. Maybe the whole idea of a gang was daft. But—

Just after tea he made up his mind and went round to Elvis's.

Chapter 21

'We have no idea where he is, Billy,' Mrs Potter said, 'he's never here when he's wanted!'

She was standing at their front door, three-quarters blocking the entrance, and scraping the last of something green and awful out of a tin-foil tray while a small army of under-nourished delivery men staggered back and forth under the weight of the new furniture.

'Like the new three-piece, Billy?' she asked, dropping the tin-foil at her slippered feet where the greyhound devoured what was left of the green and awful. 'Cost a bomb,' she said.

It would obviously survive one as well.

The new suite had an air of dumpy solidity, and it was obvious that the designer of it had been inspired by the sight of immovable elephants grazing up to their knees in heavy-weight swamp, and it was equally obvious that Mrs Potter must have borne in mind (if you could call it a mind) the prospect of the dog sicking-up again when she had selected the loose-covers as they featured irregular blobs of brown, green, and a rather unconventional purple.

Billy belted up the fronts – all the nosy neighbours squinting round the corners of their lace curtains – and turned left along the path at the top of the colliery streets.

Halfway down the spoil-heap he had to dive behind a puny birch that was struggling to hold on to life on the shaly soil.

The Gang was just coming out of the entrance to the quarry. Butch leading the way, of course, swinging his big stick. Elvis tagging along at his side, carrying the new rope-ladder under his arm. Then the rest of them, Joey talking to Little Chuff at the back.

Billy kept low in case he was seen, watching them all the time.

He waited until they were halfway to Fox-cover before he stood up.

Then he realised something.

Somebody was watching him.

He turned. It was Emma Ward tucked round the side of somebody's garage that had been threatening to fall down ever since Billy could remember.

'What you doing, Billy?'

'What's it look like?' he snapped.

He hadn't meant to snap. The words just came out like that. Sometimes, if you didn't watch out, something took over inside you.

'Can I come with you?'

He nearly snapped at her again.

Instead he nodded. He wanted to say *Yes, if you like*. But couldn't bring himself to do that.

He ran down the path, Emma following, their feet making blue quiet spurts in the shale. He felt glad she was with him, really.

Just where the path joined the Old Line Mr Fletcher's goat was grazing free. It walked a few

159

yards ahead of them along the sleepers of the
Old Line before scrambling up the bankside. It
looked down at them as they passed below. It
nodded its head, as if to say, That's right, carry
on.

Right again, mate! Billy thought. He didn't
say it aloud, though, in case Emma thought he
was crackers.

They neither of them uttered a word till they
reached the gorse bushes and then Emma said:

'I saw you having the fight the other day.'

Billy didn't reply. It took some time for the
message to sink in.

'Thought you'd spotted me at first,' she said.

'Was that you in among the bushes? I thought
it was Butch.'

'No, Butch come along ages after. Just when
you saw him.'

'Are you sure?'

'Positive. What for?'

Billy shook his head.

'Was a good fight, Billy,' she said.

'I lost.'

'I thought you were great. Nobody else would
dare do that. Not even Slattery. Know what
Slattery asked me to do the other day? Go out
with him.'

'What you say?'

'Told him to get stuffed. I don't want to go
with any lads, not yet. Not any lad, at any
rate.'

Billy didn't say anything, but he felt secretly
pleased.

Just before Foxcover they crept up the bank-side, rolled under the barbed wire, sprinted across the hardening furrow of the field, rolled under a yew tree on the very edge of Fox-cover.

They could hear shouts of the Gang gathered round the Lookout Post. If the Crag Enders were coming they'd get half-an-hour's notice. Not that they would come.

Billy and Emma dodged from bush to bush until they could see the clearing.

Butch was in the Lookout Post. He'd obviously shimmied up a rope that was still looped over the main branch on to which he was busy nailing the rope-ladder. Elvis was directly underneath him. The rest of them – apart from Little Chuff who seemed to have vanished – were grouped round, watching.

When he'd finished Butch kicked the rope-ladder and it unrolled downwards with a rush, nearly braining Elvis. He laughed.

It was made with bits of wood slatted through the twinings to make the rungs. It was pretty good, smart. They'd be able to take it up and down. Just like a drawbridge.

'Permission to come aboard, slave!' Butch shouted down.

Elvis climbed up. All the time Butch was swinging the rope-ladder about, trying to make him drop off.

'Right. Rest of you gerroff and hide in the bushes ready to ambush them! No talking! We wait for them to come.'

And you'll have a blinking long wait! thought
Billy.

But he was wrong.

Chapter 22

A minute after they'd all got settled down there was a scuffle in the bushes.

At first Billy thought it was a rabbit, or somebody mucking about.

But he was wrong about that and all.

It was Benson's big brother. People called him Tapper, because he always carried this little hammer. He swaggered into the middle of the clearing, then stopped. He was wearing a denim jacket with the arms torn off (so he could show off his tattoos), and his skintight jeans, and the big lace-up boots which he always wore.

He looked up at the Lookout Post and said:

'Which of you two's Cliffy Butcher?'

Cliff stood up on the branch.

'I am. What for? Elvis straightway started hauling up the rope-ladder.

'Wouldn't bother doing that, Titch,' said Tapper Benson.

'What for?' asked Cliffy, looking down at him. 'You'll never gerrup here.'

'Not gonna try. You're gonna come down here, small fry!'

'Sez who?'

'Sez me.'

'Not likely!' said Butch.

'What's the matter, Twit? What for you not

comin' down? You scared or something? You a yeller-belly?'

'He's not as big a yeller-belly as you!' said Elvis, who by now had tied down the rope-ladder so it couldn't accidentally fall down.

'Big gob for yer size, haven't you? What for don't you come down and all?'

'My name's Croft, not soft!' said Elvis.

'Just wait till I get the pair of you down here, Monster-mouth!'

'Anyroad, there's more than just us two, you know,' said Cliff.

'Is there? You've gorrus frightened to death, man. You've gorrus knocking at the knees! Tell you what, Yeller-belly, there's about half a dozen of your mates peeing their pants in the bushes, isn't there? Tell you what. In one minute I'm gonna go in them bushes and see if I can grab a hold of one of them. And when I do, God help him, 'cos *I* won't! Right? One. Two . . .'

Somebody did a bunk, then somebody else.

'Three . . .four . . . five .. Can you hear them runnin', Yeller-belly? That's all your big army doin' a fast bunk!'

There couldn't be many of them left now. Billy could already hear some of them were down on the Old Line clattering along it doing a fast buzz for home.

Maybe that was the wise thing to do, Billy thought. He and Emma could easily slide out backwards and get over the field, if they wanted to. But for some reason they didn't move.

'Where's all your mates now, Yeller-belly? Where's yer army?'

'Still haven't got us, though!' said Cliff.

He was right as well. He was safe as houses as long as he stayed up in the ash tree.

'Soon will have.'

'Never in a month of Sundays!'

'Wanna bet?' He dropped a gollop of spit and rubbed it into the grass with the toe of his boot. 'What's the bettin' you're down here in one minute – unless you're a coward, that is? Are you a coward, Big Twit? That's what I've heard.'

'Tek no notice of him, Butch,' said Elvis. 'Just trying to tice you down there, man.'

'I'm not frightened of that skelington!' said Butch.

'Not worth fightin' anyroad,' said Elvis. 'Couldn't knock the skin off a rice-puddin', I bet!'

'Couldn't I? Come down here and try, Monster-mouth! I'll soon knock the skin off you!'

'Don't want to get contaminated, man,' said Elvis.

'All right,' said Tapper. 'If that's the way you want it, we'll just have to do something nasty.' He looked round and called over his shoulder:

'All right, Gary! Bring out the runt!'

Gary was even weedier than Benson. He had a gormless smile on his face as he came out of the bushes dragging poor Chuffy by the arm.

Chuffy must have been keeping watch, on the edge of the wood. Probably fell asleep and they'd nabbed him.

Billy might have known it. Fancy sending Chuffy out to keep watch! What a mentality!

Poor Chuffy never looked healthy at the best of times! He always looked fit to drop. He always looked paler than pale. Now he looked two shades whiter than white.

'Don't hurt us again, mister,' he said to Benson. 'I'm sorry for what I did. I won't do it again, mister, honest!'

There were mucky marks all over his face where he'd been crying.

'Calls you "mister"!' sniggered Gary Skin'n-'bones.

'I like it! I like it!' said Benson. 'What did you do, runt? I forget.'

'I don't know.' said Chuffy.

'How can you be sorry, then?'

Gary sniggered some more, making on he was highly tickled.

'Have I to give him a Chinese Burn again?'

'Better than that!' said Benson, taking his hammer out of his pocket and going towards Little Chuff.

Poor Chuffy squealed, even before Benson touched him.

There was a clump off to their left.

Butch had dropped down to the earth.

Chapter 23

'Let the kid go,' said Butch.

'Eh? You talkin' to me? You need permission to talk to me, you know!' Snigger. 'You want the runt to go, you drop your big stick first.'

Butch dropped it.

'Better. You're learnin' fast, Yeller-belly!'

'Have I to let him go now?' asked Gary, who had lit up a fag.

Benson nodded without turning round. He kept his eyes fixed on Butch. The way he looked reminded Billy of something eyeing something up, he couldn't think what.

Chuffy belted off after Gary Fagger had booted him twice up the backside. As Chuffy crashed through the bushes Elvis shouted down at them:

'The cops'll be here any minute!'

'Oh, yeah!'

'The rest'll have gone for them,'

'Pull the other one, clothhead!'

'Fat chance!' said Fagger.

'The cops'd better come, anyroad,' said Tapper, 'because by the time I've finished wi' him over there they'll *need* to come.' His eyes remained fixed on Butch. A hard intense stare. It was a snake he reminded Billy of. A snake with something at its mercy. 'Need an amb'lance an' all!'

Snigger, snigger.

'Heard tell you bashed my kid brother up the other day?' said Benson.

'Was a fair fight.'

'Isn't what he told me. I heard you hadda get yer mates to help you.'

'I never!'

'You contradictin' me? I don't like contradictin'! That's what for I was chucked outa school!'

Snigger, snigger.

Butch shook his head. 'Was a fair fight,' he said.

'I've told you, I don't like people who contradict me – or who tell lies! Here, Gary, hold this for us.' He handed his hammer back. 'We'll use that later,' he said. 'See if we can knock a bitta sense into him!'

Snigger, snigger.

'Now we'll have a really fair fight!'

It *was* a fair fight to begin with. For the first minute or so. Benson said he was going to keep his left hand behind his back, and he did, at first,

But it was a trick really. It didn't stop there long.

Butch had managed to get past Benson's guard and landed one or two of his clumps to the chest, although he had to take one or two wallops himself.

Then just when Butch was beginning to force him back Benson whipped out his left hand and swung it round in an arc.

169

Of course, Butch wasn't expecting it. Benson's open hand caught him a real whammer right across the cheek and knocked him flat on his back into the bracken.

'I thought—'

'Never mind what you thought, kidder. This is a proper fight now! A fair fight! Gerron yer feet and fight!'

Butch got up.

And got knocked down again.

He kept getting up and getting knocked down.

It was worse than Leon Leroy and The Beerbelly With No Legs.

Billy had never seen a bullfight and didn't want to either, but his sister and Steven had been to somewhere called The Costa del Plastic and they'd seen one there. It was in an old amphitheatre where the Romans used to throw Christians to the lions when they were bored. There were still writings on the walls in the rooms under the arena where the Christians were kept, and Steven said one had read: *Christians 0 Lions 16*.

Sandra had been really upset by the bullfight. They kept sticking darts in the bull, and lances. The bullfighter was a new feller at the job, not a proper Spaniard but an American or something, and he couldn't finish it off.

They'd had to come out in the end. Sandra had felt that poorly she couldn't even go to the disco that night. She and Steven had a proper row about it.

170

'How would you like having darts stuck in you?' she shouted when she was telling them about it.

'Depends who stuck them in!' said Steven.

He was always trying to make jokes of things.

But it wasn't in the least bit funny – it had sounded really awful. . . .

And so was this.

Even Fagger had stopped sniggering and laughing now.

'Better pack up, man, Tapper.'

But Tapper wouldn't pack up. He didn't want to. He was enjoying it now. He kept bashing away at Butch, and Butch kept getting up for more. Despite himself, Billy felt an admiration for Butch growing inside him. It was amazing how much punishment he could take. At the same time he wished Butch would just lie down. But he knew that would never happen. Butch would never lie down. He wasn't the sort. That was how his brother had got the medal in the Falklands.

Maybe that information reached into the dim brain of Tapper eventually because he flung himself on Butch before he could get up, probably because he was running out of steam himself.

For a second or so he hung over Butch, pinioning his arms above his head, his chest heaving up and down while he recovered his breath.

Billy felt relieved at first. He thought it was all over.

But then things turned really nasty.

'Howay over here!' shouted Tapper to Gary. 'Give us me hammer!'

He made Fagger hold Butch's arms down.

'Now we gonna eat grass!' he said. 'Like you made my kid brother do!'

Butch shook his head from side to side.

'You are!'

'I never made him eat grass!' Butch managed to blurt out.

'I've told you once! I don't like being contradicted! You don't listen to people! See this hammer? I'm gonna start tappin' a bit of sense into your head in a minute, tough guy, but first you're gonna eat grass. Like an animal. Open wide!' He held the hammer close to Butch's head. He started tapping gently. 'You want more?' Butch opened his mouth. Benson shoved a stalk of grass in. 'Shut! SHUT! YOU WANT YOUR HEAD BANGIN' IN? SHUT!'

Butch shut.

'Now swaller! SWALLER! Better. Good boy. Now we'll see what me little toffee hammer can do . . .'

Clump!

It was Elvis who had dropped to the ground this time. He must have dropped right off the branch, there was no sign of the rope. He must have been mad to do that. Nobody normal would have done that.

'Oh, somebody else wants to play!' said Benson. 'Gerrim, Gary!'

Gary Fagger started across for Elvis. But he didn't get far. Elvis met him halfway, head down, and hit him in a very strategic spot indeed, and Fagger nearly swallowed his fag.

Thinking about it afterwards Billy was never quite sure what happened next: whether it was Emma who made the first move or him. It was likely they both moved together.

The main thing is they were both running across the clearing. Billy went to help Elvis, who was taking a pasting, and Emma went for Benson. She went for his hair, to be precise. You could tell that by the way he screamed.

Even so, even with the five of them – Daz and Joey had crawled out of the bushes (Daz kept buzzing around like an aerated flea, fists flying, not a punch landing, and Joey was boxing in a very artistic manner, without doing an ounce of damage), they still couldn't get Butch free. Maybe they never would've unless something had happened.

There was a blast on a whistle.

'Cops!' said Fagger.

Tapper paused for a moment. He had Butch's arm twisted up his back.

The whistle sounded again.

There was a sound like somebody heavy and powerful coming through the bushes.

'Howay!' said Fagger.'Run for it, man!'

Tapper pushed Butch head forwards into the grass and belted off after his mate.

A second after they'd gone the bushes parted.

Little Chuff stepped out into the clearing, this really daft grin on his face.

'Me pea must've come unstuck, Elvis,' he said proudly, 'it really blew this time!'

Chapter 24

'What took you so long, man!' Elvis said. 'Thought you were never gonna get here! Nearly hadda send for the United States Cavalry!'

He rushed across and started kicking Chuffy up the bum and they both fell over in a heap of giggles and laughs.

'What's up with Butch?' Emma asked, prodding Billy in the ribs.

Butch was bent over double. A great shuddering sob escaped him. He put his hand to his throat.

Billy went over to him.

'What's up?'

Maybe Benson had caught his throat, hit his windpipe or something. That was the first thought that came to Billy's mind.

'Eh, man?'

Another sob. Cough. Splutter.

'Butch? What's up, man?'

He still didn't answer. Billy could see his face was red as fire. Drips of blood fell on to the grass below as he coughed. He seemed to be trying to fetch something up.

Emma was coming over now.

Billy bent down and touched Butch's elbow.

'All right, Butch?'

Butch swung his head up violently. Drops of

blood went all over Billy. 'Gerroff! What you touchin' us for?' Billy could see now what a mess his face was in. And there wasn't just blood on his face. There were blotches of something else – especially under the eyes.

So Chuffy wasn't the only one they'd managed to make cry, Billy thought.

He didn't say it aloud.

'I think you ought to see a doctor, Butch,' said Emma. 'You ought to report it.'

Butch glared at her for a moment. He seemed about to speak, then didn't. Instead he turned away and stalked off, walking ram-crash through the bushes as he did so.

'Oh, man!' said Joey, when he'd gone, 'He's hurt! Really hurt. Know what I mean?'

Even Elvis and Chuffy had stopped clowning about now and were sitting up in the bracken. Daz had been trying – uselessly – to climb up the trunk of the ash tree: 'What's up wi' him?' he said.

They could hear Butch clattering along the sleepers of the Old Line now.

'Howay,' said Billy.

They all followed Butch back to the streets, keeping their distance. He left a trail of blood for them to follow.

Chapter 25

Butch didn't come to school for the next three days. When people called for him at night his mam said he didn't want to come out to play.

Elvis said it was because they'd all been cowards. They should have come to the rescue sooner, he said, before Butch got whupped.

Billy knew that wasn't right. Butch would never expect anybody to come to his rescue. He didn't expect much of other people, anyway. Probably nothing. You could tell that by the way he treated them.

And he knew he'd been wrong about the blow on the throat. It wasn't that which made Butch sob and choke.

It was the piece of grass.

The single piece of grass he'd had to chew on and swallow.

That was what Butch had been trying to bring up.

It wasn't even the piece of grass. It was the idea of it. The thought that he'd had to give in. *Hard things mend easy*: that was what his mother sometimes said. And it was like that with Butch as far as sticks and stones were concerned. But the thought that he'd had to give in – that might take a little longer for him to recover from.

'Miracles I can do today,' Steven once told Billy, 'the impossible teks a little longer!'

On Thursday two things happened. Very different. But in a way connected.

First, Butch returned to school. He rolled up in the playground just as the bell went. He sat in his desk palefaced and quiet, hardly a mark now on his face to show what he'd been through. He didn't jeer once or make any remarks at anybody. He sat bunched over his sums, doing his best in a dogged kind of way that shut out enquiries from anybody. Mrs Drury had enough sense to ignore him completely.

Second, a special assembly was called just before break.

'As some of you will already know,' said Mr Starr, 'there is a rather remarkable pea in the boys' toilets—'

(Not me this time! Elvis told Billy.)

'—and I am giving strict orders now to all and sundry—'

(The well-known firm of solicitors!)

'—That nobody is to touch it.'

(Yuck!)

'Who said that?' asked Mr Starr.

Elvis looked round and pointed at the back:

'Somebody back there, sir!'

Mr Fixby marched up to a big lad – any one – and marched him off to Siberia. He always got his man.

'Now, about this sweet pea,' said Mr Starr.

('Told you it wasn't mine,' said Elvis.)

* * *

178

At break-time there was practically a queue outside the boys' bogs because everybody wanted to see the remarkable pea.

'First time in me life I've had to queue up for one,' said Elvis. 'Are they charging for admittance?' he asked a lad just coming out.

'Not that I know of.'

Mrs Drury even went in to see it (they all had to cross their legs and wait outside) and when she emerged she said it was A Miracle of Nature.

What it was, was somebody had dropped a pea down the sink-hole of one of the washbasins and it had taken root in the U-bend and somehow managed to thread its way up the pipe and through the metal grid, and now it was rearing its tiny head in the smelly air of the toilet.

'Hardly seems worth the effort!' said Elvis.

But it did seem a bit of a miracle to Billy.

They were just going out when Butch came in and shoved his mouth under the tap of the next basin to get a drink of water. He stood up, mouth full of water, and for a minute Billy expected him to spit on the plant. But he didn't. He just looked down at it, swallowed, then went out.

Billy knew then that Butch still wasn't functioning right. Normally he'd have had a good go at doing it in. He remembered the frog down at the marshes.

Outside in the yard it was even more obvious Butch wasn't his normal self. He didn't punch a single soul or make anybody carry him on their back.

He didn't even kick anybody up the backside as they walked past – a really bad sign.

And when Elvis went cringing up to him and asked him if he fancied a ride Butch didn't even laugh. He just looked away. He looked mad.

He kept that up all day. And at night he wouldn't come out again.

It wasn't till Friday afternoon break that the change came.

The rest of them were having a kickabout when Emma seemed to mis-kick(?) the ball and it happened to go straight to Butch who was propping a wall up.

At first it looked as if he wasn't going to join in. He just looked down at the ball for ages. Then he bent down and picked it up. At first Billy thought he was going to fling the ball at them, hard. That probably was what was going through his mind. But he didn't. He dropped the ball at his feet – he almost grinned – and started dribbling the ball towards them.

Butch wasn't the world's Number One dribbler. He could hit a ball. When he took a shot from near-in and if he connected, the kid in goal – provided he had an iota of intelligence – dived the wrong way pronto – for the good of his health.

But dribbling was another matter.

Nevertheless, as he moved goalwards, one after another seemed confused by his brilliance, his fancy-dandy footwork, and slid the wrong way or too late – even Daz had the sense!

When Butch shot, the tennis ball spun off the front of his trainers in a hopeless spiral, no power behind it at all, but Joey dived the wrong way all the same, and Elvis just had time to deflect it in accidentally (??) while apparently (???) trying to clear the line.

'GREAT GOAL BUTCH!' they all shouted.

He almost smiled then.

And last period in the afternoon when Mrs Drury announced that Billy had won the essay competition – she was William Robinsoning this and William Robinsoning that for twenty minutes – Butch never looked round once in his jeery way.

In fact, when he did look round, when everybody had stopped clapping, he winked at Billy, like a real mate, and smiled.

And Billy felt an immense sense of relief flooding over him. He winked back at Butch and smiled broadly.

He felt he was back in the Gang again now.

He felt they both were.

Chapter 26

It was a cold clear night when Billy went out into the back yard to fill the coal bucket, before *The Bobby Downes Spectacular* started.

The Arab had been on the Nine O'Clock News again. His men were being evacuated by French warships to another country where, for a while at least, they'd be given refuge.

Maybe that was just the way things were on this earth.

He opened the coalhouse door: it was pitch dark in there.

They *were* shutting down Steven's Colliery in Barnsley. Mr Potter had been right. They'd just had a letter that morning. They'd all been offered other jobs, in other pits. Steven had been offered a job near Cardiff but he wasn't taking it. Next time it would be Timbuktoo, he said. After that, The North Pole. They were coming back home, he said. Back where they belonged.

That at least had cheered up his mam. Though what they were going to do for a living they hadn't a clue.

Billy groped about till he found the shovel and started filling the bucket.

The factory was shutting down as well. Krapp Ringhorn Spitz were setting up a new factory, in South America, where the wages were cheaper. They'd just given it out on the local telly. And Mr Hyslop had resigned from the union and was on his way into the EEC as a Euro MP. Surprise move Lord La-de-dah had called it. Mr Hyslop was interviewed in the studio: he had a collar and tie on and was struggling to grow a moustache. Billy's dad had nearly fell off his chair with laughing.

'I fail to see what there is to laugh about!' Billy's mam had said.

'You have to laugh woman! If you don't laugh in this world, you cry!'

'And you're surely not going down that Club tonight? Not after you've lost your job?'

It was the finals of the pools championships tonight and Billy's dad was in charge.

'It'll mek no odds if I stop home, pet.' he'd said. 'Life must go on, Alice.'

'Life!' she said. 'Is that what you call it?'

But she had been pleased about Billy winning the essay competition. She'd stuck the book token up on the mantel shelf where everybody was sure to notice it if they came in.

'I particularly liked the fight scene,' Mrs Drury had said. 'It was almost as if you'd been in one yourself, William.' And she'd looked at him in a funny sort of way. 'And the word "carnage" that you used. That's the kind of vocabulary you should aim for in future. Where on earth did you get it from?'

'From telly, miss.'

That had made Emma smile, and Mrs Drury disappointed.

'And do you know what it means? Anybody?'

'Miss!'

The Soskiss, of course.

'It means like meat, miss. It comes from a Latin word.'

'Absolutely right, Samantha. Two house points. The latin word *carnaticum* just as a matter of interest.'

('Me brother 'as one an' all,' muttered Elvis.)

Fancy Soskiss knowing that, though, Billy had thought. She really was a brainbox. It was no wonder people said she found playing the fiddle that easy she could do it on one leg!

He'd gone up to her after and said he was sorry she hadn't won.

'Hard cheese,' he said.

'In my opinion yours was better, Billy,' she said. 'It was definitely more – imaginative.'

Always a mouthful.

She'd blushed as well. Billy wouldn't have thought her capable of blushing. She'd looked down and fumbled with her pencil-case that nobody on this earth was allowed to touch or she'd report them to her mother and the FBI. When she dropped the whole lot on the floor Billy bent down and helped her to pick them up.

'Thanks, Billy,' she said. She blushed some more then.

'Some people are at last learning some manners, I'm glad to say,' said Mrs Drury, and she really smiled at him.

Billy thought he'd better get out.

He'd done a fast bunk into the yard where

Emma and the rest were waiting to play football.

Billy paused in filling the coal bucket to look up at the stars.

There were a heck of a lot of them up there tonight. A few Billy had never noticed before. Maybe somebody had made a few extra?

And the funny thing was, they were always there, in the same place, and yet always moving: were they, too, part of Mr Starr's famous wheel?

And could they really be responsible for deciding whether you broke your neck next week or broke The Bank at Monte Carlo instead, as his grandma believed?

And what about Mrs Drury? Was she right?

Maybe the Greek gods really were up there scratching their heads and wondering what to change themselves into next – white bull, swan, duck, gerbil, guinea pig? – when they next came down to earth in The Big Lift to do a bunk with some poor feller's wife.

Maybe Jason and his Argonauts really were up there, rowing forever across endless seas of emptiness. Or Cadmus and his Merry Men – merrily sowing the dragon's teeth that would one day spring up as fully-armed warriors ready to hack and slash and plague the life out of some poor souls down here on earth who, if the truth was known, already had enough on their plate to cope with.

Warriors reminded Billy of Butch.

And the single piece of grass that had floored him. Knocked the stuffing out of him in a way that blows never could. Made him sob.

A knockout in the fourth round, by a single piece of grass!

Billy smiled in the dark.

He shovelled more coal into the bucket.

How funny Butch had been those first two days back at school. Almost human. The way he hadn't dropped a gollop of spit on the pea-plant.

Nice, really. But definitely not himself.

He remembered the way Butch had smiled when he scored The Worst Goal of the Month. The way he'd gradually come alive after that.

Like the film Billy had just seen on the Potters' new video about this monster with a six-inch bolt through its neck that this feller in a white coat like an ice cream man shot a current of electricity through that had made the lights go out all over Europe and he'd sat up and said *Master! Master!*

They'd been so glad when Butch'd become himself again. They all had.

You didn't like Butch. He wasn't the sort you liked.

You either hated his guts or worshipped him. It depended which side he was on at the time.

But it was funny how after his whupping they'd all come nearer to liking him than they'd ever done before. Almost as if by being whupped he'd become one of them – almost.

Which, in a way Billy couldn't quite make

out, made being whupped like some sort of – good thing?

The coal bucket was full now.

He went indoors. He put some coal on the fire and the flames sprang up hungrily.

He went into the kitchen where his mam was sitting.

'Fancy a cup of tea, Mam?'

'I wouldn't mind, pet.'

He made it for her, then went back in the other room and sat in his dad's chair, close to the fire where it was warm.

The Bobby Downes Spectacular was just starting and a lot of girls with plastic vine leaves in their hair were being pursued across a lawn towards some trees by Bobby, a manic look in his eye, as if he couldn't wait to get his hands on them.

In a moment the very opposite would happen and Bobby would emerge from the trees being pursued by the girls and, this time, running for his life.

It was all daft really.

Or was it? Was it really that daft? When Billy remembered what had happened in the last two weeks he thought maybe it wasn't as daft as it first seemed.

His mother came in with her cup in her hand. 'Not this Tommy Rot again!' she said as Bobby burst out of the trees. But she sat down on the sofa to watch all the same. She smiled at Billy and her eye took in the book token on the mantel shelf as she looked across at him proudly. 'Lovely cup of tea, Billy,' she said.

'Is it, Mam?'

He smiled across at her. He leaned back in his dad's chair and prepared to enjoy himself for a whole solid hour. He felt comfy inside, and warm.

And the comfort and warmth inside him – Billy knew – arose not only from the fire.

If you would like to receive a Newsletter about our new Children's books, just fill in the coupon below with your name and address (or copy it onto a separate piece of paper if you don't want to spoil your book) and send it to:

The Children's Books Editor
Transworld Publishers Ltd.
61-63 Uxbridge Road,
Ealing
London W5 5SA

Please send me a Children's Newsletter:

Name..

Address...

....

....

All Children's Books are available at your bookshop or newsagent, or can be ordered from the following address:
Corgi/Bantam Books,
Cash Sales Department,
P.O. Box 11, Falmouth, Cornwall TR10 9 EN

Please send a cheque or postal order (no currency) and allow 60p for postage and packing for the first book plus 25p for the second book and 15p for each additional book ordered up to a maximum charge of £1.90 in UK.

B.F.P.O. customers please allow 60p for the first book, 25p for the second book plus 15p per copy for the next 7 books, thereafter 9p per book.

Overseas customers, including Eire, please allow £1.25 for postage and packing for the first book, 75p for the second book, and 28p for each subsequent title ordered.